EVERYONE REAPS

The Turner Family Drama Series

Part One

DESHANA L.WRIGHT

Copyright ©2024
All rights reserved. Written permission must be secured from the author to reproduce any part of the book.

Printed in the United States of America

ISBN: 979-8-3305-6275-6

10 9 8 7 6 5 4 3 2 1

EMPIRE PUBLISHING
www.empirebookpublishing.com

Dedication

This book is lovingly dedicated to those who love me, encourage me, motivate me, and inspire me to do better everyday! Life is always changing; and those who are on the journey with us now, may not have been before, and may not be forever. With that said I'd like to give special flowers to each of my children starting with:

Jazmyne Rogers- my firstborn, best friend and ladybug... Thank you baby for being my loyal helper in this life, my rock, shoulder to cry and lean on so many vulnerable times when I needed your parenting instead of me being the parent! In all your wisdom you have taught me so much! I am forever grateful.

My second born Daughter and baby girl- Kandyce Rogers: Baby... You have made this trip so fun, intriguing, enlightening and wonderous! We are two sides of a coin for sure! I love how you teach me new things and help me expand my consciousness in mind blowing ways! I love you for life!

To my firstborn Son Christopher Wright Jr. Son... I am so so proud of you! I mean it when I say that I look up to you! You have motivated me and inspired me in ways i could not have imagined! To have become a Sherriff Deputy, and show'em what the good guys are about? That is a shining example of my awesome seeds' achievements. I love you so much.

Finally, Last but never least; my baby boy Roman Wright... Son you are so special to me in so many different ways... you remind me of all the best parts of your Dad and myself combined! Your level of strength and determination, your hustle and drive is so inspiring from my view and I am so so proud to be your Mom! When I see you working hard to complete something you have started it fills me with so much pride and joy, I am overloaded with happy expectations for the future!

I would also love to thank my Baby Brother Edward Charles Davis Jr. (Jr to us) who has always been my best friend in this adult life, gives the best advice and will ride at dawn with no hesitation if I need! I love you bro... My younger sister Sherita Davis who is my bestie and day one, loves me and is a constant supporter, inspirator, and voice of reason... I love you Sis! Thank you so much!

To everyone else who wasnt mentioned... I know who loves me! You make sure that I know it and I am forever grateful! This dedication is meant for you as well!

Thank You for walking alongside me in this journey. I wish us all wealth and abundance. We are creators... Let's gooooo!!

Preface

"As you grow, you learn." That statement is simple, but yet oh so true. You learn about people and experiences. You learn about good and bad, right and wrong, fair and unfair; the difference is how it all makes you feel or react. The challenge seems to be what type of person you will still be or become once it's all said and done.

Will you still be the type of person who is able to be depended upon and called upon after you have been used and taken advantage of repeatedly? Will you still be a sweet and polite person after you have been mentally and emotionally abused because of it? Will you still be a greedy and stingy person after you have lost everything because of how you were?

These are questions that a person must seriously consider. It is hard to place yourself in a situation if you feel like it doesn't pertain to you, but as life goes on, things happen, times change, and people change. Life takes place. However, I can tell you one thing that does not change for some reason. I don't care who you are, what you are into, how you do it, or why you do what you do... You Always Reap What You Sow. What goes around comes around, so if you can, try to do right, and then only right will come back to you!

Chapter 1

2000

Iesha Turner was 5'4, weighing 135 pounds, with a shapely and curvaceous body. At the young and exciting age of 21, she knew she was beautiful and eagerly looked forward to the rest of her life. Her skin was the color of hot chocolate. She had bashful, mesmerizing hazel eyes surrounded by long, wispy eyelashes. Iesha wore her eyebrows carefully arched, and her skin complexion was so flawless that she did not need make-up. She possessed an almost perfectly shaped set of snow-white teeth within her bright smile that bore deep dimples on each side of her face and made you feel as if she kept juicy secrets. She stylishly sported her natural long, dark brown hair that was manageable- yet coarse and thick. She loved wearing her hair nappy because it gave her a sense of pride in her black heritage and extended more definition to her apple-shaped face. Her ears were draped with costly golden hoops that twinkled and glittered when the light bounced off them. She also wore a thick gold herringbone necklace that rested just above her cleavage and placed undeniable emphasis on her breasts. She kept her fingernails and toenails manicured with the latest airbrush designs and sequins.

It was her normal routine to visit Lynn's Nails every other Saturday morning, where she was known as a regular. Iesha held a standard that would never allow anything but expensive name-brand clothing to touch her body. She regularly sported high-priced fashions such as Gucci, Prada, and Dolce and Gabana.

She coordinated her outfits with Coach, Fendi, and Louis Vuitton handbags, hats, belts, shoes, and accessories. With a single glance, you could see that Iesha took great pride in her appearance and that she was very materialistic. She often referred to herself as single, sexy, and free. She had never had many female friends due to jealousy being a part of the relationships, usually from the other party, but she had always had several male friends ever since she was a child. Outsiders may have called Iesha promiscuous, but she thought of herself as more of a free spirit than anything.

Iesha did not like restrictions and was upfront enough to let it be known. She would let all of her guy friends know that she is free to talk to or keep company with anyone she chooses, and she will not be held by any titles or to anyone. Iesha was strong and independent; growing up poorly taught her to get what she wanted for herself and not to look toward anyone for anything. But in this day and age, where most men were usually leery of "Gold diggers or Leeches," Iesha's independent nature was more than a fresh drink of water to most of the men she met; it was highly intriguing and respectable. She had become that way after graduating from high school and getting a taste of what it was like to be able to buy anything her money could afford.

Iesha would often sit back and reminisce on her rough childhood; she was aware that her materialistic lifestyle had developed from growing up as a poor and deprived child in the slums of Newark, New Jersey.

1982

As the middle child of four, she hardly received any attention and could count the times on one hand that she had received anything brand new. Her mother, Sheilah Turner, was doing the best she could by trying to raise her children all by herself as a separated, single parent on welfare.

Usually, the new clothing and shoes (if there were any) were given to Iesha's older sister, Tish, and then passed down to her once they didn't fit anymore. Tish, who was three years older than Iesha was more like a mini version of her mother. Tish was a natural-born leader and supervisor, so she did an excellent job keeping her three younger siblings in line. Iesha had so much love and respect for her older sister, but sometimes, she would find herself feeling anger burning from the growing resentment of being bossed around so much. However, she did find it comforting and thought of her big sister as a blessing in her life. Tish was always giving Iesha whatever shirts she could not fit anymore, as well as socks, pants, shorts, and, on several occasions, even underwear.

Iesha, in turn, would have to pass down her outgrown clothing that looked as if it could be for either boy or girl to her two younger brothers, Dante and Damion. She had grown accustomed to doing without things and being told "No" at a very young age; it taught her not to ask for anything. Iesha had decided within herself way back then that if she could not get whatever she wanted for herself, it wasn't worth having.

Iesha could not shake the painful memories of being teased in school for sporting second-hand clothing and cheap shoes from the local Goodwill store. "Bell bottoms, we know you wear 'em Bell bottoms, why don't you share 'em!!" That was the painful song that was forever engraved into her memory that the cruel school children had actually gotten together and made up about them after an incident in which one of the popular girls' recognized her former jacket being worn by Iesha. Alisha Willis didn't spare a minute telling the entire fourth-grade class that her parents had given the jacket to Goodwill last summer.

While the other kids were being dressed in Levi Jeans, Starter jackets, and Nike, Addidas, or Reebok shoes, Iesha and her siblings had to make due with second-hand bell bottom jeans that had scrub marks on the knees, butterfly collar shirts, or turtle necks, that was way outdated, and shoes such as Pro-wings or Coasters which everyone knew came from Payless. What everyone didn't know was that on the very few occasions when Sheilah would find the Pro-wings or Coasters at the thrift store, she considered it a steal and would "Jump on them," as she would commonly say. Sheilah considered it a small privilege for people to assume that she even had the money to take her kids to cheap Payless rather than always being known for shopping at Goodwill.

On the few occasions when Iesha and her family were out shopping, if she complained to her mother that she didn't want a certain shirt or style of pants because she was going to get teased at school, she would be answered by her mother glaring at her, smacking her lips, and saying "Girl, you better be glad you gettin' anything. You must be crazy to act like you too good for these clothes, you know I'm doin' the best I can off our budget. You better act like you appreciate it 'fore we walk up outta' here without YOU gettin' nothin'. Don't mess around and make me slap you!" Iesha's mother would roll her eyes and stroll down the aisle with her wide hips brushing the clothes hanging on both sides, all the while still talking about it and shaking her head, obviously bothered. "Got the nerve to complain to me, like we got money growin' on trees or somethin'. Better hope I don't jump on you fore' we get up out this store! Better shut up and be happy."

Iesha would hide behind her older sister as they all trailed their mother down the aisle; for some reason, it seemed that if her mother didn't look back and directly see her face, she would get over her angriness quicker. Iesha would fight back the tears that were welling in her eyes and threatening to spill over onto her cheeks at any given blink; she knew the danger of being seen crying after she had just gotten clowned by Momma; that would get you a for sure slap in a heartbeat cause Momma didn't play. Neither did Momma care who was in the store at the time or if they were looking or not, and she carried the attitude that she dared them to say anything about her disciplining her children. She felt that it was her God-given right.

Iesha could also recall times when her mother would take them to visit their cousins or other family that they didn't get to see that often. Momma would give them a speech that lasted the whole bus ride there. "And don't be askin' for none of they food- I don't care if you do get hungry, ya'll will eat when we get back home. I ain't tryin' to hear from the rest of the family that I brought ya'll over all hungry and stuff like I don't be feedin' ya'll or somethin'. That's the last thang I need is somebody talkin' about us. Understand?" "Yes, Momma." All of the kids would respond in unison. "Even if they offer you somethin' to eat, don't take it cause they don't mean it- and don't nobody ask me if ya'll can spend the night cause you know you can't, I'm tellin' you right now don't even try it, cause the first one that do is gon' get popped upside they head, do I make myself clear?" "Yes, Momma," The kids replied again. Momma would go on and on, rattling off a long list of rules she expected to be followed during their rare visits and the after threat of what would happen if the rule wasn't followed.

Momma would do anything from slapping you in the face or upside your head to taking off her shoe or her belt in public and beating you with it. Iesha could not help but twist her mouth up in disgust at the painful memories of her childhood. She loved her dear mother to death, but she did carry a small amount of resentment for her at the harsh treatment that she'd endured as a child.

Iesha recalled how before she became a single parent, when Iesha's Daddy D'wayne still lived with them, Momma was a much sweeter person.

The Turner family used to attend Sunday morning and Wednesday evening services at the Holy Temple Baptist Church on Edgar Lane. Daddy was deeply religious; he had been raised in the church as a child by his parents. Daddy would commonly refer to the church folks as his "family." He had been around most of the members his whole life. He had the reputation of being a very faithful member, and although Sheilah had not ever been to church before she met D'wayne, she tried to be as faithful as she could in going for her husband. Early Sunday mornings, the children would be awakened by the sound of Momma singing "Amazing Grace" and "Welcome Holy Spirit" as she cooked pancakes, sausage, grits, and eggs.

It was so warm and comforting to be awakened to that atmosphere. The children would brush their teeth, wash their faces, and go eat breakfast. Afterward, they would all put on their neatly pressed dress clothes, which Momma had laid out the night before. Daddy would come out of the room smelling like the scent of Old Spice aftershave, looking so handsome in one of his neatly creased, 3-piece Sunday suits. The family would all load up in the long, boxed-shaped Chevy, which also served as Daddy's work car, and head to the church. They would walk into the small church and embrace the sweet sound of the choir singing and praising The Lord.

Iesha vividly remembered how she would feel a tingle on the surface of her skin and warmth all over her body at the sound of the praises. Daddy would say that feeling was the presence of "The Holy Spirit." Iesha loved going to church and always listened carefully to the messages; she would even bring her notebook to write down scriptures to read later. After church, they would come home, and Momma would cook Sunday dinner—fried chicken with Momma's delicious homemade gravy, smothered potatoes, cornbread, and steamed cabbage. Daddy would lead them into a prayer of thanks, and they would all sit down, eat, talk, and laugh.

It seemed to her that they were all so happy back then. Iesha remembered another memory of how sweet her mom used to be once when she was invited to a Halloween costume party by one of the other little kids at school when she was in the second grade. She had mentioned the party to her mother but had expected her to say no, she couldn't go because they couldn't afford to buy a costume. However, Momma had surprised her; she smiled at little Iesha and said, "Baby, what do you want to go as?" Iesha smiled and thought dreamily, "Uuuuhhhhh...a princess! I wanna be a princess!" Momma said, "Okay then, we just gon' have to find a way to make my baby a princess!" When Iesha got home from school the next day, her mother had a pretty little pink dress laid out on her bed, with pink stockings and white patent leather shoes. A little sparkly crown was embedded with diamond sequins and glitter forming the word "Princess," laid right beside the dress.

Iesha shrieked with delight, "Ohhhhh, Momma, thank you so much! Thank you! Thank you! Thank you! I love you, Momma." Iesha turned around and hugged her mother the tightest and the longest she had ever hugged her in her life. Momma laughed as she hugged her back, "Don't forget to thank yo' father, he's the one that went into his savings so I could buy it." She would never forget that day. That was one of the few days she could ever really remember being made to feel like she was something special. Iesha would bring that day to her remembrance to remind herself that her mother really did love her in the cold days that followed once her daddy left.

Iesha was never really sure about all the reasons why he left, but she was aware of the problems between the two of them. Sometimes, late at night, when they thought all the kids were asleep, Sheilah and D'wayne would stay up in the living room arguing. It was usually about her accusing him of being with someone else. Iesha recalled that her Daddy would deny it over and over: "No Sheila, I wasn't with nobody, baby. You know I be workin' hard all day and I can't help it if I smell bad by the time I make it home. Won't you give me a break? I'm tryin' my hardest to do you right, woman!" Daddy would sound as if he were pleading. Momma would angrily growl back, "You aint s'posed to smell like that! Oh, and don't thank fo' one minute that I don't be seein' Susta Rose Anne lookin' you all up and down at church every Sunday, you must thank I'm blind, you must thank I was born yesterday, yeah, I know what time it is- but you just let me catch you and see what's gon' happen!" Daddy would retort with, "You just don't know that you gotta good man, do you? I work every day and put in all my overtime to take care of our family, and you just keep accusing me of nonsense! I'm gettin' tired Sheilah- I aint gon' take this too much longer. You ain't gon' miss yo' water till the well run dry, girl; you just watch and see!" They would argue until early in the morning or until Daddy finally gave up and just stopped talking back.

The next morning, however, Momma would be in the kitchen cooking breakfast and singing to herself, while Daddy would be at the table reading the newspaper and drinking his morning cup of coffee, preparing to leave for work. They would act like everything was so fine to the point that Iesha would sometimes wonder to herself if she had been dreaming the whole thing, either that they had found some way to make up quickly, or they were putting on an act believing the children didn't know they had ever argued in the first place, Iesha reasoned. This arguing and making up went on for years before Iesha's Daddy decided he'd had enough.

D'wayne had struggled within himself to stay and take it as long as he could; he was trying to live as God wanted him to, and he knew that The Lord's word said, "Do not divorce, except for cases of sexual immorality," and also that "If an unbelieving wife is willing to dwell with you then do not divorce her because she is sanctified by her believing husband, and by this, the children are also made holy." D'wayne was certain that Sheilah wasn't cheating. He was sure that no other man would dare go for her nonsense. D'wayne had felt he'd done all he could to keep his marriage together, but he just couldn't please Sheilah anymore. When it reached the point that D'wayne felt miserable every day and dreaded coming home from work, he knew that he had to do something. He had threatened to leave many, many times before, but this time was different. He was beginning to hate Sheilah. He loved his children with all his heart, and they were the only reason he'd endured this pain and torture for so long, but now, even his love for them was not enough to keep him in this bottomless pit. He didn't have the heart to look Sheilah in the face and let her know he was really walking out on her and their family, so he waited until she fell asleep one night and, snuck out of bed, quickly packed all of his clothes in a suitcase, and left silently in the middle of the night. He left a note on the kitchen table, which served as a final goodbye before walking out the door.

Once he got in his car, he headed south to Decatur, Georgia, where his parents had settled years ago. He felt that he could at least get his head together down there. Maybe he would come back one day, maybe not, he thought as he drove away. Tears streamed down his face as he imagined the hurt and pain he was going to inflict on his children by leaving. One by one, he pictured each of their faces... Beautiful, Smart Latisha, Cute, Adorable Iesha, Strong, Independent Dante', and Wise, Inquisitive Damion. It was almost enough to make him turn around and try again, but then he pictured Sheilah's bitter, scowled-up face with her constant false accusations, and it made him smash on the gas pedal accelerating a little faster. All D'wayne Turner knew that he needed peace of mind and was fed up with being mistreated. Although he loved his children more than anything else in the world, he felt that one day they would surely understand why he left; no one could ever rightfully say that he did not try hard to make it work. So, with that assurance in mind, D'wayne headed steadily down the interstate, never to look back at Jersey again.

Chapter 2

1984

When D'wayne finally reached Georgia some 9 hours later, he safely arrived at his parent's huge home. He settled in and was able to clear his head. Within days, he felt more at peace than he had felt in years. Within weeks, he had started a new job at the local Military base stationed in Atlanta, and now he felt like he had a whole new life. He thought about his children every day and even thought about calling them, but he knew it would only complicate things.

Within six months, D'wayne met a young lady named April LeBeau. She was like a morning breeze in Dwayne's eyes. He had tried to deny his feelings for her in the beginning, knowing deep inside of his heart that the rightful thing to do would have been to divorce Sheilah before he called himself moving on, but with April being his across the street neighbor and with her family having close family ties to his parents for many years, it made it all the harder to avoid her or stay away from her. After trying to resist his feelings of wanting to be loved and overlooking his own deep loneliness, he gave in and allowed April to come further into his life. He began to experience life as he had never known it before. He had been transformed from a family man, father of four, and faithful husband of 13 years into a bachelor, a single black (and still young) man with no family ties or responsibilities. He was free to do as he pleased with no explanations being owed to anybody.

D'wayne found himself loving life in a way that he never thought possible. He was now beginning to see what living a new carefree life was like.

He began to date April, and within eight months, they were engaged to be married. D'wayne found himself at a point in his life where he simply began to block out all memories of his other wife, kids, job, neighborhood, and even life itself; it was easier that way. His parents had never approved of Sheilah, and they encouraged him to move on. His former family was now the newest Turner family secret to be swept under the rug as D'wayne. His parents agreed to stick to the story that he had been serving in the Military overseas and was fresh back home from Kuwait, so by 1986, within two years of leaving his family behind, D'wayne had married April. They had given birth to their first child, a baby girl named Destiny. She was 14 months old, and April was about four months pregnant with what she had hoped to be a baby boy.

April considered it a blessing that she met a man like D'wayne. He was sweet, charming, handsome, and truly a Southern gentleman in every sense of the word. She was so excited to be married to such a wonderful man and ecstatic to begin a long, loving, and enduring lifelong relationship with her new husband and children; from April's standpoint, nothing could be more perfect. As time passed and April was now in her eighth month of pregnancy, she was both joyfully and anxiously anticipating the birth of her brand new baby boy; although her feet were swollen, her legs and back hurting every day, she was more than grateful and appreciative of her new family. Life could absolutely be no better for her at this point. April and D'wayne had agreed that the little one would be a Jr., rightfully named after his daddy. April would sometimes take special note of how

D'wayne would rock Destiny to sleep, singing her lullabies at bedtime, laying her clothes out for the next day, and even helping April with fixing Destiny's hair on occasion; he was proving to be the perfect father, especially for his first time. April was now sitting in the living room of the small two-bedroom cottage that the two now shared; they had already been making plans to move to a bigger home, possibly before the baby was born. D'wayne was now working a Military dispatcher position at the local base; as far as April had been informed, he was just working this temporary assignment until he happened to be stationed at a new base; at that time, he would either have to move his family with him wherever he ended up being stationed next, or they would have to wait for him to come back home; all depending on the length of the assignment.

D'wayne had made this all clear to April before they had married that he was a Military man. If he had to be shipped out at any time, he could not be hindered by his family and them being the reason for him turning down any Military assignments that he was to be placed on. D'wayne, however, made it clear to his new wife that she would always be provided for no matter what, and also, no matter how long any assignment he was sent on may last, he would always return to his lovely wife and his children. So that was the understanding that the two held, and D'wayne had counted it a blessing that his new wife was not the argumentative type; he would often think to himself that this is what he needed all along; a good down south country-fed girl who knew how to appreciate a good man, with no back talk or nonsense in the equation. April sat on the couch, rubbing her swollen belly and lightly pressing down on certain areas where she knew the baby's body was resting. It gave her such a thrill to feel the baby actually shift positions inside of her; she knew him so well that she had his routine down pat already; she would know when he was sleeping when he was stirring around, and even when he was satisfied from eating the food which she nourished them both with and then he would actively move about and rotate inside of her for hours on end. Her husband was enjoying time to himself out on the patio out front; D'wayne sat on the porch, lost in thought for the time being. Most of the time, his new life was enough to keep him content and eagerly looking toward his future, but on this night, he was bothered.

The date was February 25th, and it was Damion's 6th birthday. This had been on D'wayne's mind all day long; it was still so hard to really be gone from his wife and kids back in Jersey, and sometimes it still felt like he was living a dream or even an alternate reality that he could snap out of whenever he wanted to, but of course, the true reality was hitting home fast that he had created a very complicated situation out of things and for himself, and going back home would not be that simple. D'wayne had to fight himself all day long from calling his baby boy to tell him a happy birthday; he found himself wondering, questioning, and reminiscing on all the birthdays that he had shared with his children and wife in past times. He knew that Sheilah had more than likely made his son's choice of birthday cake, whatever it happened to be this time, and bought his favorite flavor of ice cream for the celebration. He almost felt as if he were there in spirit as he looked at his watch, noting the time to be 8:32 p.m., he wondered within himself if maybe they were celebrating at this very hour and singing happy birthday as his son joyfully blew out his candles on the cake. This thought left a great sadness in D'wayne's heart; if it had not been for his four children, whom he loved so deeply, it would have been nothing at all, just to forget about Sheilah.

The thoughts of his children pulled at his soul so overwhelmingly that he sat there strongly wrestling with the idea of driving up to the gas station and using the pay phone to call home and at least tell his son happy birthday. He silently debated back and forth, "I can't just call them after being gone all this time; what will my babies think? Well, at least you would be showing them that you still care and that you will go for something one day." His mind and subconscious went back and forth for a while before he decided to get up and go. D'wayne had gathered all of his courage and was going to go and do the right thing regardless of the complicated situation that he was now living in, but just as he had stood up from his patio chair, April spoke out from right behind him, startling him. "You finally ready to come inside and keep us company, Sweetie?"

D'wayne snapped his head around to look at his wife; he was a little irritated at the sweet southern twang that she held in her voice that he normally took comfort in; however, at this moment, it jerked him from his thoughts, which were already as heavy as a steel weight around his neck. He gazed into her face as she leaned against the doorpost, her head slightly tilted, still rubbing her watermelon-sized stomach. D'wayne just watched her for a second without commenting as he marveled at her beautiful features, just like always.

April was quite the opposite of Sheilah, and D'wayne was grateful for it. She was a petite, high yellow woman, standing at about 5 foot even with freckles and beautiful sandy brown naturally curly hair. She held a very sweet disposition, and seemed for the most part completely innocent in her ways. D'wayne was only the second man that April had ever been involved with in her whole life, the first man whom she had been engaged to marry before him, was killed in an automobile accident and April had been left to grieve for three whole years before she met D'wayne. At the young age of 28 years old, she still had her entire life ahead of her, and she now looked forward to spending every last day of it with him. D'wayne could not resist the wide smile that began to spread across his face at the sight of his lovely wife, she had no way of knowing about the horrible position that she had put herself into by being simply put: in the wrong place at the wrong time in life. D'wayne always found himself wrestling with mixed emotions these days, one minute he was fine, happy and content, and the next minute he was feeling guilty and confused, on the brink of confessing the entire scandalous secret of his other family to April, but he knew that he could never bring himself to hurt this delicate God-send of a woman that he had been blessed with; he would rather die first. April stood in the doorway and watched her husband in a loving way, she knew that he had a lot on his mind these days with the pressures of them expecting the new baby and also having to move soon, and not to mention the fact that he could be uprooted and expected to change work locations at any time with the base. Most of the time when April was able to sense the tension that her beloved husband was feeling she would just come up behind him and begin to massage his shoulders and back, and rub his forehead in a soothing way which was symbolic of her rubbing his worries away. It seemed that the two held this little silent agreement which would usually end with them in the bedroom making long hours of sweet love to each other and not discussing any of the problems or worries at hand. April silently noticed the way that D'wayne had seemingly slipped back into his thoughts even though he was gazing directly at her, it was almost as if he were looking right through her.

She gently offered her company again, "Baby? ... ... You alright? You need to talk to me about somethin'? If so, I'm right here….." April held a concerned look on her face; she did not like all of the stress being placed on her husband this way. She was currently on maternity leave from the cook's position that she presently held at Briggsmoore Elementary School, which was less than one block away from where they now lived. She often found herself wishing that she could somehow make enough income for the both of them and the two children to where D'wayne could just quit the Military position and therefore remove the threat of having to move away, possibly without them. April had always told herself that if that situation came to pass, she would be as strong as possible, but on the inside, she prayed to God every day that her family would never be split apart, not even temporarily. D'wayne found his words and responded, "Oh no baby, I am just fine... Just sitting out here enjoying the peace and quiet of the cool evening and just relaxing….how's my sugar plum doing? Are you feeling okay?" April smiled at D'wayne as she welcomed his warm words. Moving closer to him, she reached up and wrapped both arms around his neck, planting a small kiss on his lips. "Well, let's see here, mister, I am bloated, oversized, and uncomfortable, but nevertheless, I got Liver and Onions simmering on the stove. Destiny has already eaten and been bathed. Now she is knocked out, and I am prepared to do you the same way, feed you, then knock you out! So how bout' it? You hungry?" D'wayne laughed at his wife's light humor; it was all a part of what made her so sweet and special in his eyes. She was a good woman, and it was not her nature to gripe or complain about anything; she always did her fair share, and no matter how difficult things were, she made the best of life in every situation. He reached down and returned her embrace by grabbing her around the waist and holding her close to him. He planted soft kisses on her cheeks and neck as he caressed her back gently. After a few moments, he tiredly responded, "Baby, you don't know how good your home cooking sounds to my hungry gut at this moment! Go on and hook it up, girl; get it ready for me, and I will be in right away, okay?" D'wayne began to release his embrace as April turned to go back inside, "Alright baby, comin' right up!" She smiled as she waddled back into the living room and down the hallway toward the kitchen. D'wayne stood on the porch a few moments more so that he could mentally collect himself and push all thoughts of his son and other family out of his mind once more. He would not go and call them, and perhaps it was better this way; after all, it may only add to the already existing and no doubt still fresh pain that his children were still feeling at his sudden leave of absence, so to speak. He would see them again one day; that was why he had lied and pretended that he could be moved at any time with his current position; he had fixed it that way so that if he decided to leave to go and see his children, he would be able to have as long as he needed to take to mend loose ends. He had kept the possibility tucked into the back of his mind that sometime after his baby was born, he may be able to use one of his 'passes' to go to Jersey and buy a motel for a few weeks, and from there, go to visit each of his children at their schools and maybe even pick them all up from school to spend time with them and not have to hassle with even laying eyes on Sheilah. He was unsure how his children would regard him with how he had just up and left them. When he got the chance to see them again, he would thoroughly explain why he had to leave their mother and also clear up any misclarifications so that they would know that it had nothing to do with them whatsoever. He even fantasized about telling them all about their new sister and brother and new stepmother; he knew all the while that this part of the fantasy would never be anything more than just what it was, a fantasy. He could never reveal the truth about his whereabouts; he would have to come up with some other lie and add to the already gigantic-sized snowball of lies that was slowly piling up and heading for some invisible, unseen collision that lay up ahead. D'wayne Turner put all of these thoughts out of his mind as he turned and opened the screen door, stepped into his new home, and made his way toward the kitchen where his hot dinner and beautiful wife awaited him.

Chapter 3

Iesha often thought about her father. On one occasion, tears began to well in her eyes as she thought back about the morning when they all realized their Daddy was gone. She remembered how they all woke up, as usual, to get dressed and leave for school when they noticed that their Daddy was not in his usual place at the table reading his paper. Momma was not cooking breakfast and was seated at the table, dressed in her terrycloth house robe with a cup of tea in front of her, and her eyes were red and swollen from crying. Silence surrounded her and sent a thick vibe through the air, letting the children know not to ask any questions. After thirteen years of being a close family, they never saw or heard from their Daddy again.

Iesha was left to grow up with a bitter attitude that forced her into an endless battle of proving to herself and others that she was someone who was worthy of being spoiled and given top priority. She made up her mind that she would always have whatever it was that she wanted, no matter what it happened to be. Iesha made sure that she got good grades in school despite her lack of friends due to her poorness. She always kept her future in mind and promised herself that she would never have children unless she could give them the best of everything. To Iesha, "everything" included a good, hard-working father, a big, nice, beautiful home, and all the brand-name fashion clothing and shoes they ever wanted or needed. She constantly dreamed of having a family and being able to give them all the things she and her siblings were denied of having.

She graduated from high school at the top of her class and immediately began to work. Iesha took on two full-time jobs throughout the week and part-time courses at the local college campus on the weekends. She was majoring in Real Estate and had long-term dreams of owning her own housing company, which could provide new homes to underprivileged families on a low income. Iesha was an overachiever and wasn't satisfied with her success until she knew whatever it was that she was attempting to do was as close to being perfect as perfect could get. Iesha worked from 6:00 in the morning until 1:00 in the afternoon at the Coffee House Cafe' in the mall. She worked hard in the little restaurant frequented by teens and young adults most of the time. She would voluntarily come in thirty minutes early and leave thirty minutes late, never including the extra time on her time card. Putting in extra time earned her the title of "Employee of the Month" over and over for eight months in a row. Her other job was maintained at the Food Mart off 65th Avenue and Jefferson Court. Her shift began at 3:00 in the afternoon and lasted until 8:00 p.m. Iesha prided herself on never being tardy or absent from work, although she knew she was taking on more than the average person could handle and stick with. Within one year of working, she moved out of her mother's house and into her own apartment. She made enough money between her two jobs to pay her rent and utilities, keep her refrigerator and cabinets stocked with plenty of food, maintain her car note, buy all the expensive clothes and jewelry she wanted, and still be able to put away 200.00-300.00 dollars off of each check. Iesha was very happy with her success.

After two years of consistent hard work at the Food Mart, she was promoted to assistant manager and attained status as a hiring counterpart. Now, she had a say in who could get a job there. For Iesha, this was more than she had ever hoped she'd accomplish while still being so young. When Iesha would come home to her cozy two-bedroom apartment after her long work day, she always felt a burst of joy and gratitude, knowing she could immediately slip out of her clothes as soon as she walked through the door and not have to worry about anyone else in the room with her. Every night, as she made her way to the bathroom to take a hot shower before going to bed, she was reminded of the small, cramped three-bedroom 1, one-bath cottage she grew up in across town. In Momma's house, there was no way you could just take off your clothes and feel free to walk to your room naked; there was always someone else around- and besides that, you would probably get beat all upside your head for trying to pull a move like that. She had to share a room with Tish, and Damion and Dante' had to share the other room. The last room, the biggest of all the small rooms in the house, was Momma's room. Now that Iesha was gone, needless to say, Tish was ecstatic about having her own room for the first time in years, and Iesha was just as grateful to be giving it to her. As Iesha let the steamy water run over her tired body, she tried hard to push the negative memories of her childhood out of her mind. She tried to focus on all of the good things she had accomplished. She turned off the shower and stepped onto the lush, dark green bath rug in front of her bathtub. She had decorated her home in lively colors. It always brought joy to her soul when she looked at the decorations of her first home outside of her home. The bathroom walls were wallpapered in a pattern of green and pink watermelon slices on a pink background. Watermelon, which was Iesha's favorite fruit, was the theme for the entire bathroom. She had hunted the department stores until she found a watermelon-shaped soap dish, a watermelon-striped toothbrush holder, pictures of watermelon patches being grown in the hot summer sun, and one of a little black girl eating a slice of watermelon and smiling. She had also found some green curtains that matched perfectly with the rest of the green accessories in the bathroom. Complete with a pink and green face and hand towels, watermelon-scented hand soap, body wash, and air fresheners, the bathroom was the perfect expression of something that made her feel happy. The bathroom was just one example of how the rest of Iesha's apartment was set up. She had decorated her kitchen with a theme of country peaches, her living room in plum colors, and her bedroom resembled a box of Valentine's Day chocolates. She wrapped herself in a big, soft green bath towel and made her way to her bedroom down the hall; while passing the second bedroom she had designated as a guest room, she briefly looked inside to ensure its cleanliness. The guest room was the only plain room in the house, containing only a twin-size bed with tan linens and a small oak dresser. Once entering her bedroom, she sat on her plump, Queen-sized pillow top bed and began to lotion her body with the Watermelon Peach body cream she had purchased last week at Bath and Body Works. Her sore muscles began to tingle from relief as she slowly massaged each part of her body. She pulled back her red silk sheets and climbed into bed. Pulling the thick red and pink comforter up to her chin, she snuggled into her warm bed, and with a small smile, she visualized what she would be wearing the next day; within a few minutes, she sank into a deep, relaxing sleep.

Chapter 4

2000

Juwan Phillips, a.k.a Joose, had tried and tried to find work but was repeatedly denied. Joose was caramel-complexioned, handsome, tall, and muscular-looking. He wore his hair in cornrow braids and had a mouth full of gold teeth that sparkled and glistened every time he smiled or spoke to anyone. He gave off the appearance of a gangster, and he was comfortable letting his pants sag below his butt, openly exposing his Hanes underwear for all to see. Joose had been dressing this way almost his entire life, so he didn't see anything wrong with it. Part of his everyday apparel was a wife beater tank top underneath an open plaid collar shirt, along with his sagging jeans, and his white Nike's. Joose was only twenty-five years old but he had already experienced more things in this life than some people double his age. He had a hardcore look in his eyes that made you feel as if he did not trust you and, in turn, that he may not be trustworthy either. You could look at him and tell that he had done prison time before. He had served time for crimes such as Armed Robbery, Drug Sales, and Assault with a Deadly Weapon. In the hood, he was well known for putting in work; if you asked about Joose, everybody knew who you were talking about.

On this particular hot, humid August afternoon, Joose strolled toward the bus bench on the corner of Marcus Lane and 5th Street, feeling angry and disappointed as he left from yet another failed job interview. This was at Robert and

Associates, an insurance company on 3rd Street. He had been considering applying for a while because he felt like it would sound good to be able to tell folks he worked at an insurance company; it just sounded important to him. He walked through the door at five minutes to 2:00, hurriedly sat down, filled out his application, and briefly straightened his clothes. He made sure he was finished by 2:00 on the dot, which was the time his interview was scheduled for. He had a good feeling about this; it felt right in his gut. He looked up as the white man in the neat business suit came out and firmly shook his hand. "Hello, Juwan, my name is Mr. Bradford; please step into my office," he smiled. Joose gave Mr. Bradford a quick once over, noticing his expensive 3-piece Armani suit that was neatly creased and his polished black patent leather shoes that appeared so shiny he wondered if he might be able to see his reflection in them. Mr. Bradford had recently gotten a trim on his hair and a salon shave Joose observed as well. He could see that this man was very well off and probably had little to no financial worries. Somewhere in the back of Joose's mind, a mini-movie played out of him following this man home late at night and shoving a gun to the back of his head, forcing him inside and robbing him at gunpoint, tying him and his wife up, gagging them both, and emptying their safe which was probably filled with thousands of dollars, expensive jewelry, and antiques, but as quick as the thought had come, it faded away, as Joose reminded himself that he was a changed man now and he was trying to do better. He stepped into an unusually large office and was set up more like an apartment than a working office, he thought. As he stepped inside, he noticed how plush the Burgundy wine-colored carpet felt underneath his feet. He quickly scanned the large paintings of waterfalls and tropical scenery that covered the cherry-toned walls of the office. A placard directly behind Mr. Bradford's chair held a quote that read: "Most people don't plan to fail; they just fail to plan." That statement echoed in Joose's mind, and it seemed it was somehow written just for him. He couldn't help but admire the cherry wood and burgundy color scheme that looked to have been carefully thought out. The two chairs seated directly in front of the highly polished cherry wood desk were custom-designed in burgundy velvet that perfectly matched the carpet and encased with the same cherry wood trim as the desk was made out of. The comfortable chairs looked like a welcome mat to legs that had been walking all day like he sometimes had to do. To the left of the desk was a matching couch and loveseat positioned directly in front of a window seat with a view of the city landscape. As Joose allowed his gaze to trail out the window, he looked at the breathtaking view of the seashore, which was lined by the expensive suburban homes that filled this nice area of New Jersey. In the middle of the living room scene sat an antique oak coffee table with an array of magazines organized down the middle and a bowl of peppermints and other assorted candies resting on its top. Joose found his gaze slowly wandering around the room as he drank up every detail of the place. He found himself wishing he were here alone so that he could take his time to enjoy looking at all the small details that had been put into the room's decoration. His eyes trailed to the right of the living room scene, and behind Mr. Bradford's desk, they fell on a large aquarium containing around ten to fifteen brightly colored tropical fish. Further to the right, an outstretched bar with three fancy barstools occupied the other side of the room, and he was sure that it held nothing but the richest of wines and whiskeys inside. Right next to the bar was a chrome refrigerator and matching microwave, and right beside a sink served as a small kitchen area. Mr. Bradford said nothing as he watched Joose drink in the details of his cozy, homelike office. When Joose finally looked back to Mr. Bradford, he felt that the man was used to this reaction from applicants and whomever else he invited to this place. "Please, have a seat," Mr. Bradford said calmly as he motioned to one of the chairs while still holding Joose's gaze. Joose was good at reading facial expressions, a skill he had learned in prison. As he took his seat and looked into Mr. Bradford's eyes, he realized that while looking around and admiring the office, he had also been thoroughly looked over without even being aware of it. Mr. Bradford was doing a lousy job of trying to mask a disdainful look in his eyes and a scowl around his mouth as he looked Joose in the eyes. After a few moments, Mr. Bradford attempted to correct his expression with a phony smile. Joose knew right then and there that he would not get the job. Mr. Bradford extended his hand, reaching for the application, "Let's begin, shall we?" He tried to calm himself and gather his words as he saw Mr. Bradford's gaze come to a halt at the mid-section of the application. Joose knew what was coming next. "Tell me a little bit more about your felonies, Mr. Phillips?" Joose was silent for a second, trying to think of a good way to tell his story as Mr. Bradford watched him expectantly. "Well, Sir, In my youth, I was a little hardheaded........" Joose tried to hold his gaze steady, "I never had much as a child, and so I began to go down the wrong path: dealing drugs and robbing folks...my felonies are for 3rd-degree robbery and drug sales." Seeing a look in Mr. Bradford's eyes that looked something like revulsion, he quickly tried to clean up the chance that he knew he had already blown. "I am proud to say, though, that I have successfully obtained my G.E.D, and I am tryin' to change my life for the better. I want to work and be responsible, and if you give me a chance, I will be one of the best workers you've ever seen. I won't be late, I'm very responsible ... and I will make you glad you hired me, Sir; all I need is a chance." Joose smiled, revealing a mouthful of gold teeth, hoping it would soften his appearance. Mr. Bradford was silent for a while as if thinking it over, then responded dryly, "We'll call you, okay?" Joose knew that meant "No." He sat there watching Mr. Bradford as he folded the application closed. Joose rose from his seat when he spoke again, "Sir, at least tell me now if you're not going to give me a chance. I would appreciate your honesty, just as I have been honest with you." Mr. Bradford looked up at Joose, obviously surprised by his statement, and took a small breath as his ears began to turn red. "Juwan, I have several more applicants for this position to interview. I am not prepared to answer now, but I appreciate your honesty and will consider that when I make my final decision, okay?" Mr. Bradford cleared his throat and stood to his feet, non-verbally, ending the interview. He extended his hand to Joose and stated, "I will call you either way, alright?" Joose accepted the handshake and returned with one of the firmest grips he could give, hoping that it sent a message of trustworthiness to Mr. Bradford. He turned and walked out without another word; inside, he felt like crying.

As he neared the bus bench, he racked his brain, wondering why life had to be so hard for him. He guessed that maybe it was because he displayed an image that looked too much like the projects where he was raised, and he was certain it was because of the trouble on his criminal background record. Joose sat down on the bus bench;

reaching into his front shirt pocket, he pulled out his pack of cigarettes. He did a quick count of his pack before pulling one out, lighting it, and inhaling deeply, allowing the nicotine rush to calm his nerves. Tomorrow would be two weeks since he had been released from the New Jersey State Penitentiary. He had promised himself that this would be his last time, no more in and out. One of his parole conditions was that he had one month to find some kind of employment and be able to show he had a legal source of income. Finding a job had proven harder than he thought it would be. He had no work history, and if that wasn't bad enough, he noticed that after mentioning his felony, the interviews usually ended abruptly. If it weren't for the promise that he made to God that he would try to do right this time and become an upstanding, law-abiding citizen, he would have already copped a zip of Cocaine and began his hustling again. As Joose thought of all these things, he got lost in his thoughts.

1992

The thugs and gangsters that ran the Garden Projects had become just like a second family to Joose. When his father died right after his 11th birthday, Joose felt like his whole world had ended. Without the extra income that Joose's father brought to the table, his mother couldn't handle paying the mortgage on their home and all the bills, along with the credit card debts, which were left unpaid at the time of her late husband's departure.

Anita had done everything she could to keep the beautiful home that her hardworking husband had poured so much of himself into, including working any overtime available at the Sweet Creek Medical Facility, where she was currently employed as a nurse assistant. She even tried to take on a part-time job waitressing, but that ultimately left her too burned out to spend any time with the two boys that she was now struggling to raise all by herself, so she had to quit her second job and hope for the best. Ultimately, the family was faced with having to give up their home and move into the only place they could afford at the time; the notorious Garden Street Projects, which were well known and feared by their reputation for heavy drug activity and gang violence; but Anita Phillips could not afford anything better and therefore was left with no other choice.

At the young age of thirteen Joose started running with this kid named Curtis who was selling drugs on a daily basis, and not much older than he was. For some reason Joose looked up to Curtis, he was young and independent just the way Joose wanted to be. Now that his father was gone Joose was left with no one to look toward for direction. Curtis was sixteen and seemed to have it going on. He was fitted head to toe every day with different colored pairs of Nike's and Jordan's. He wore brand new pressed Levi 501 jeans with coordinating NFL jerseys to match his shoes. He kept his hair in a fresh neat haircut which he got done at the barbershop once a week. Curtis told Joose that he could put him in the position to start making money, and get him hooked up with no problem at all. Joose wanted all of the luxuries that he noticed Curtis having: money, clothes, girls, popularity, he even had his own car, a red 1990 drop top Ford Mustang sitting on 18" gold rims-all at the age of sixteen! It seemed like just the solution that he needed to repair his poor and homely reputation. He also thought of how he could give his mother some money to help her out because she was struggling to raise him and his baby brother Terrance all by herself. Curtis told him that the way he made his money was that he was part of the G.P.M., Garden Projects Mafia, and that Joose would have to join too, if he wanted to be a part of what he was doing. Joose had noticed the huge gang of thugs hanging out all the time, some posted up drinking while others were shooting dice in the corner by the dumpsters. There were usually females hanging out too, and they wore red all the time. No matter what time of day or night it was they would have a boom box out side blasting rap music that you could hear throughout the entire complex. Joose would sometimes lean out of his bedroom window and strain his ears to hear what the dirty lyrics of the music the gangsters were blasting was saying. They would stand in the back of the projects in the parking lot as cars would pull up, and beep their horns. Each thug would take turns going to make silent transactions at each car. There would be a brief exchange of one handing the other a fistful of something and then the car would pull off. Joose's mother had always warned him not to talk to the gangster's because they were "bad news".

They gave the apartment projects a bad name because the group of gangsters would start fights with anyone who walked through the apartments if they weren't from Garden Projects. It was a well-known fact that if you didn't live in Garden Projects or you weren't coming to buy drugs, you better not step foot into the apartments. Joose's mother always said that if she were able to work more hours at her job and save the money, she would move them out of there, but unfortunately, they were stuck there for the time being.

Joose vividly remembered how he had thought about all the negative things he had heard his mother saying about the gang as he considered joining it. All the times that he'd seen his mother gazing out of the window with tears in her eyes as another homicide story featured on the evening news with Garden Projects as the scene of the crime; yellow tape decorating several sections of the apartments that they knew as home was just a normal thing. He knew what he was considering doing would be a big disappointment to his poor, hardworking mother and break her heart. He thought he would have to keep it a secret from her as long as possible. As he thought back, he could see her face in his mind's eye. He weighed up his options, keep momma happy by going through school and getting good grades quietly until he was old enough to get a job, keep living poorly and getting barely acknowledged, or take a risk and start enjoying fast money, popularity, nice clothes, cute girls, and street status. Joose chose the latter decision. He made the choice that forever changed his life; he decided to join the gang and made his decision known to Curtis the next day.

After his mother would leave for work every day it was his routine to walk his little brother Terrance to the bus stop on the corner and wait with him until his bus came; and then he would leave walking by himself to Mike Eddings High School around the corner where he attended 9th grade. Only recently and behind his mother's back the last few months he had began waiting for Curtis to pick him up after he put his brother on the bus. On that day, after the bus picked up Terrance, Joose stood there waiting for Curtis with his heart pounding as he thought about the reality of his decision. Pretty soon he would be a part of the G.P.M. No longer just normal old Juwan Phillips. Pretty soon he would also be a part of the vicious clique that his mother despised so much. Just then Curtis pulled up, "Wutup Dawg!" Curtis called. As

Joose stepped off of the curb and into the fancy car and sat down, he strapped on his seatbelt replying, "Ah nothin' man, Im just thinkin' hard about the offer you made me yesterday, that's all". Joose closed the car door and leaned back against the seat. Curtis eyed his young friend up and down, "You look like you hecka stressed, wasup wit you?" He smacked loudly on a toothpick in the corner of his mouth and displayed a sideways sneer before continuing. He cocked his head to the side, then said with an attitude, "Look son, I was just tellin' you what it took for me to get as far as I am in the game, but now, if it's stressin' you all like that, then don't even trip on doin' it, stay broke, hell if I care, that's on you, kid". Joose stared at Curtis. He looked at the gold rings studded with white diamonds on each finger of both hands, he looked at his black corduroy jeans and red K-Swiss shoes that were neatly coordinated with his red and white Chicago Bulls Jersey. He had his outfit topped off with a red Chicago Bull's baseball cap flipped around backwards on his neatly faded haircut, and a thick gold rope around his neck that was probably worth more than him and Terrance's entire wardrobe put together. Joose reluctantly said the words that he would later regret a million times as he pictured himself not having to suffer with being deprived anymore, "Okay Curt, count me in."

Chapter 5

As he remembered it, the rest seemed no more than a blur. That day after school, instead of going home where he knew Terrance was waiting, he headed toward the back of the apartments with Curtis at his side. To join the gang, he had to get jumped in, which meant he had to let about ten thugs fight him at one time. He was scared but did it because he knew he had to. He just kept telling himself it would be over before he knew it. The whole ordeal lasted maybe ten minutes, but it felt like hours. The females were in the background cheering on the rest of the gangsters, "Go Ray Ray, tear him up!! Show him what G.P.M is all about!!" Another girl screamed, "Yeah, Big Mike, do him dirty!!! Show him wasup!!" It felt like he was being beaten to death as blows landed one on top of another to his head, face, arms, legs, and chest. In his defense, Joose began to swing back blindly. He had never been into a street fight before, so he just repeated what was being done to him. He felt his fists land on two or three faces, but it seemed as if fighting back made them attack him harder. As the pain began to worsen from rapid punches and obscenities coming from all angles, Joose just gave up. Once he fell to the ground, one kick after another sent torrents of pain to his stomach, back, legs, and head. He felt an explosion, which caused him to scream as a fist collided with his nose and sent a waterfall of blood gushing down his face. His lips were swollen, and both of his eyes were swollen shut. Just as blackness began to close in on him and he was almost unconscious, he heard a strong male voice speak from the crowd, "That's enough!! The lil' homie is cool- back up offa' him, he's in."

All Joose could do was lie there. He felt as if every bone in his body were broken; his first thought was that he must have been crazy to agree to this. He was in so much excruciating pain that he was sure he must have come close to being killed. He felt a pair of strong hands pull him to his feet. "Shake it off, lil' homie, shake it off; you took it like a real "G," you alright? What they call you?" Joose cracked open his swollen eyes as much as possible and looked up into the face of a man he would later look up to like a father. "My name is Juwan, but my nickname is Joose." He answered through big, swollen, bleeding lips. 45-year-old Willy Banks, better known as Doctor Willy, looked down at Joose, smiling, "Okay Joose, that's yo' hood name then."

Willy turned to the crowd of gangsters and loudly announced, "Listen up, Garden Projects Mafia...This right here is Bloody Joose; from now on, he is to be referred to as our family. If anybody got fonk wit this one right here, they got fonk wit all of us- understand?" A big round of applause and cheers rang out "Yeah, that's right,.no doubt,..fa sho'..." were the responses from the huge, rowdy clique. Joose formed a smile on his swollen, disfigured face at his acceptance from the gang and at the fact that his life would be different now. He couldn't wait for it to begin.

"Screeeeeeeech!!" The loud sound of the bus braking in front of Joose snatched him from his memories. He quickly flicked his cigarette butt over his shoulder and stepped onto the crowded bus, paid his fare, and made his way to an empty seat near the back. He was grateful to have a seat to himself; being fresh out of the joint, he wasn't comfortable with sharing his space with strangers yet. As the bus slowly pulled away from the curb, Joose laid his head back against the seat and allowed his gaze to drift out the window at the low-budget buildings that lined this end of 5th Street. As the bus picked up speed, the broken down neighborhood, liquor stores, prostitutes, raggedy cars, and homely people strolling the street all began to blur together while Joose took the occasion to rest his eyes and appreciate being out of the sweltering heat for his 30 to 45-minute bus ride home.

Joose's mind drifted back to the past; suddenly, it seemed as if the bus, people, and noisy chatter were non-existent. Joose stood in the doorway of his apartment in Garden Projects. His white T-shirt was soaked with blood. His face was horribly disfigured, to the point that he resembled a monster from a horror movie. He felt at that moment as if he were in a horror movie. He had already prepared the lie he was going to tell his mother. He would say that he got jumped on the way home from school by some thugs. The scenario vividly unfolded in front of him as if he were in the first row of a drama play.

"Joose...Joose, is that you, honey?" His mother called out as she approached the living room from the kitchen, wiping her hands on her apron. She was in the middle of asking him why he was so late and telling him dinner was almost ready when she saw his face; she stopped dead in her sentence and dropped the plate of dinner rolls that she was carrying. As the glass shattered all over the floor with a loud smash, Anita began to scream "Oooohhhhhh, Ohhhhh my God!! What happened?? Whoooo did this to youuuuu? Ohhhh...Ohhhhhhhh!!!!!". Joose could never forget how his mother was shaking and screaming as she grabbed him while she cried, asking him what happened to him. Her love for him brought tears to his eyes, and he joined in her crying out of the guilt of the pain to come that he knew he was going to put her through. As he told her the story he had rehearsed, he felt sick to his stomach from his deceitfulness. He had never lied to his mother like this before. His mother believed him and did not doubt him; she brought out the first aid kit, a warm washcloth, and an ice pack and began to nurse his wounds. He stayed home for two days while his mother took care of his hurting face and applied the medication necessary to quickly heal the swelling and bruising. On the third day, his mother insisted he stay home, but Joose said he had to be at school for an important test he needed to take.

He left early that morning, but he didn't go to school. Joose headed straight to the rear of the apartments where his new family awaited. When everyone saw him approaching, they sent up a cheer of applause welcoming him, and to Joose's shock, a small group of thugs actually headed over to him to meet him, hugging him and pounding their fists on top of his, showing him love. Joose felt such acceptance from the clique that he began to feel like he must have made the right choice. One of the other guys walked up to Joose and said, "Hey Lil Joo, Doctor said to have you go see him when you come through." "Cool, where he be at?" Joose replied, trying his best to sound like a real thug. "He in numba 26". Joose headed toward the apartment marked 26 near the end of the apartments where the gang was gathered, and he knocked on the door.

Immediately, somebody snatched the door open and stuck a loaded gun to Joose's mouth. Joose's eyes grew large as he anticipated the loud bang he was sure would follow, and he thought he was about to be killed. A mean, dark-skinned face glaring back at him snarled, "Nigga, who are you?" Joose was so scared that his words wouldn't come out, just then Doctor Willy appeared behind the man with the gun. "Chill out, Black, that's the new lil homie Joose; he cool, let him in." The man with the gun, Dirty Black, lowered his weapon while eyeing Joose warningly. He slowly stepped aside and let Joose pass. After Joose stepped inside, they closed the door and locked it, "Next time, you better knock with the Gangsta Code, or else you might get yo' cap peeled, Lil Nigga!" Dirty Black announced as he looked Joose from head to toe. Joose looked away from Black and toward Doctor Will, "One of the homies said you wanted to see me." "Yeah, Lil Man, come sit by me..let me give you the rundown. I need to fill you in on what's expected of you from our family and what you got coming from us."

Joose spent the entire day with the Doctor and began to feel comfortable with him right off the bat. Doctor Willy began by introducing Joose to Dirty Black, "Joose, this here is my right-hand man, Dirty Black. Now, you can call him Dirty, or you can call him Black, but whatever you do, don't call him out his name because he just might kill you." Joose looked over at Black sitting on the couch in the living room; he was sneering at Joose and nodding in approval as if the Doctor speaking of him being a killer were a compliment. "You are gonna learn a lot of street politics by being a member of our mafia, but one of the first is that you must prove your loyalty to the hood. All of your brothers' and sisters' have been through the same kind of initiation that you are going to be put through, 'cause before we have your back to the fullest, we gotta see what you about, understand?" Joose nodded in agreement as he listened to the Doctor's rundown. For hours, the Doctor talked of the consequences of being a snitch and the "Don't talk, don't ask, and don't tell" policy of their hood. He spoke of being willing to die for one of your brothers or sisters and how they were truly his new family, with Doctor Willy and Dirty Black being known as the Fathers of the hood or the "O.G.'s,"

Original Gangstas. Doctor Willy finished running down the rules and politics of the hood; then, he began to explain the different hustling methods that the hood used to make its money. Joose felt his adrenaline flowing with excitement as Doctor spoke of him being taught how to sell drugs, steal cars to be sold to the black market, rob people, and even learn how to be a Pimp and sell Prostitutes. Everything Joose heard went against the morals and values taught to him by his mother, but Joose was strangely attracted to the thought of living a criminal lifestyle.

As the days went on, Joose began the slow but definite transformation from an innocent schoolboy to a young, disrespectful gangster. It took his mother a while before she confronted him, although she noticed the change almost immediately. Joose thought that he was really hiding his new lifestyle from his mother by going to school during the day and hooking up with the Doctor and the clique after school while his mother was still at work. He had figured that he would still try to keep his grades up and good attendance at school so that his mother would not be alarmed or know anything unusual was happening. Anita, however, knew her child much better than that, but she was not the type of woman who jumped to assumptions. She just continued to watch before saying anything. At first, she believed that Joose was going through puberty and experiencing his manhood, then she started thinking that the change in his mannerisms had occurred as a result of the beating he had taken when he was jumped. She knew she was right about the change in his attitude being linked to that incident somehow because he had changed so much since it happened. Anita was unsure what to think or how to go about confronting him, so she decided to investigate him a little bit more to find out what was going on for herself.

It was a Friday morning and Anita left out of the house, on her way to work as usual (or so Joose thought). Anita had started her car, and pulled out of the apartments, but instead of heading up Maine Street like she usually would have done to go to work she just parked in between some other cars lining the street, in an angle to where she would be able to see Joose as he left the house and walked to school. She watched and waited and finally she spotted him. Anita could not believe her eyes. She knew that it was Joose because he was walking Terrance to the bus stop, but he was not wearing his normal school clothes that she had bought for him. She watched her son in shock as he walked beside her other son dressed in a bright red sweat suit, with a red bandana tied around his head. He was wearing a pair of black shoes with a bright red Nike sign that she could see even from a distance. As she looked on at her son with her mouth hanging wide open, trying hard not to believe her own eyes, she began to feel queasy at the stomach as she realized that he was dressed very similar to the thugs that hung out behind the apartments. As Anita began to calculate her new arising assumptions she continued to stare in disbelief as she tried hard to convince herself that her innocent Juwan would never betray her in such a way as this. There must be some other explanation as to why he was dressed this way. Anita had the strongest urge to just drive up and confront her son right then and there, but her better judgment told her to watch him and try to learn more. She sat and watched as the school bus arrived at 8:15 and picked up Terrance. Anita continued to watch as Joose stayed at the bus stop after Terrance was already gone. A knot began to form in her stomach as she thought about how school started at 8:30, and she wondered why he was just standing there. Just as she was about to turn the key in the ignition to drive over to him she saw a red drop top Mustang pull up in front of her son and saw him jump into the passenger side door with a wide smile on his face. Anita felt like she was playing the role of a private investigator as she waited for enough distance to pass before she began following the car. She was not prepared for what she would witness today. Joose had made plans to engage in the final task of his one month initiation today, he had not planned to go to school.

Joose had already stolen two cars for the family, he had robbed an elderly man at gunpoint as he exited the bank, and he had purposely engaged in a high-speed chase with the police in a stolen car to prove that he could get away if he were ever caught in the middle of committing a crime. Besides everything else, Joose had already been taught by Doctor the basics of selling drugs and was now selling them before, during, and after school to make his money. He had already attained a good portion of hood status by outrunning the Highway Patrol on his very first try, which was something claimed to be nearly impossible by the clique, and he had also beaten the elderly man after he took his wallet. He didn't want to do it, but he wanted to be respected and feared early on so he wouldn't have to fight the gangsters again to prove himself. He overheard one of the older G's talking about him after that incident, saying, "Oh yeah, Lil Joose, that nigga is crazy. He aint got no heart, I know he's a killa- you can see it in his eyes!" For some reason, that piece of acknowledgment made Joose feel good, and it also made him thirsty to be known as one of Garden Project's most dangerous thugs.

Today, however, would be his final day to prove how ruthless he could really be, and he planned to do something that nobody expected. Joose's final assignment to end his initiation was to rob Chang's Food and Liquor Market on the corner of Thomas and 33rd Street. No one had ever successfully robbed the store without being apprehended. The story told to Joose from Doctor was that the Asian family who ran the store also lived in an upstairs apartment over the store. Anytime a robbery of their store occurs, the cashier sends some kind of alert to the upstairs occupants and stalls the robber while they are still bagging the money. When the robber finally exits the store with the money. Usually, two or three people are waiting near the exit to grab the unsuspecting robber, wrestle him to the ground, and hold him there until the cops arrive. Doctor told Joose that attempting to rob Chang's Market was a part of everyone's initiation but that everyone so far has made the sacrifice of going to jail in the process. In Joose's mind, he was set to make history from this robbery. He had made up his mind that he was going to kill anyone who got in his way. In Joose's reality, his actions are symbolic of a video game or a movie, and he is the star. He did not feel any remorse for his actions because he felt that he was only doing what needed to be done. As Joose and Curtis drove up Thomas Avenue, nearing the liquor store that sat on the corner ahead, Joose had an uptight stomach as he pictured himself murdering someone for the very first time. Curtis handed him the 38-Special revolver, the same one that he had used to rob the old man; he looked it over then shoved it into his waist as he reminded himself that he was the main character of this action movie and that after today, he would be looked at as one of the "G's" who would make history for Garden Projects.

Anita continued to follow Joose and Curtis at a 50 to 75-foot distance, and she made sure that she was not able to be spotted but at the same time, able to keep the car in plain view. Something in her gut kept telling her that she should drive up on the side of the red Mustang, flag the two young boys down, and snatch her son out of the car to take him home and talk to him- but she decided that she wanted to observe, and find out what her son was up to. Curtis pulled the car to a stop on the curb, which lined the street on the side of the store. He sat there for a moment in silence before he spoke to Joose as if giving him one final chance to back out of it. Finally, Curtis spoke, "Well, Joo, It's all on you now, homie; I'll be sittin' here waitin' on you, but if they get yo' ass, I'm drivin' off-- I'm just lettin' you know wasup right now, you better make it quick, and if you get caught up you bet' not mention my name, ya dig?" Joose glared back at Curtis, realizing he expected him to get caught, "Fa sho' man, you know I aint no snitch! Watch and learn, son!" Joose said with a small grin. He jumped out of the car and ran into the store; Joose yelled, pulling out his gun, "Gimme all yo cash right now, and if you move yo hands anywhere besides that register, I'm gon' pop you!! Give it up!!" The small Asian lady paused for a minute from fright, then proceeded to open the register and bag up the money. Joose noticed that she seemed to be going slower than she should have, so he kept looking around in nervous anticipation, thinking that someone would probably come through the doors any second.

Joose decided to fire a warning shot to make the lady hurry up. "Blappp!!!" The loud sound of the gunshot rang out, "I said now, Bitch!! Hurry up!" The lady shrieked and ducked, putting her hands over her ears as the bullet ricocheted from behind her and hit the glass countertop, splitting the glass and shattering it to pieces. "Okay, Okay, I give you all the money, just don't kill me, please." She yelled and pleaded. She then began to bag the money much quicker, which satisfied Joose. When she heard the gunshot, Anita was just pulling in three cars behind Curtis' Mustang. "Oh my God...." She yelled as she tore off her seatbelt and jumped out of her car; she ran toward the store, not knowing what awaited her; all she knew was that she had heard a definite gunshot and that her baby boy was inside this store.

As Joose thought back, it seemed like the whole scene played out in slow motion; he grabbed the bag of money from the woman and began to run toward the door; he was sure that the woman's family was waiting outside the door for him so he steadied his gun in his grip for preparation to shoot whoever was on the other side. As he exited the store door, he saw out of the corner of his eye a dark figure reaching for him; with zero hesitation and on impulse, he aimed and shot twice, "Blapp...Blapp...." He ran two more steps before his mind began to process what was going on; he swung around, mouth dropped wide open in horror as he recognized the beautiful face of the person who was now bleeding from the chest and slowly sinking toward the ground, still reaching out toward him. "Ma!..Maaaaaaa!" Joose screamed. His eyes were huge as he watched his mother fall to the ground in what seemed to be slow motion. Tears began to burn and well up in his eyes as he dropped the gun, then the bag of money, and fell to his mother's side. "J...Ju.." Anita gasped and croaked, trying to call her son's name one last time; she strained, trying to reach up and touch his face, as blood began to spill from the side of her mouth and blackness began to close in on her. "Maaaaaa!!! I'm so sorry, please don't die!! I'm sorry...Please.." Joose begged and pleaded, but he realized within himself that it was too late as Anita went limp in his arms with her glazed eyes staring up blindly into and beyond her son's face. Joose sat frozen in place, holding his mother's head in his lap as the tears streamed down his face while he wailed, screamed, and cried out loud, temporarily forgetting that he had just committed an armed robbery and was still on the scene.

Somewhere in the distance, the sound of a siren began to whine. Joose could only hold his mother's head in his lap while rocking and crying, covered in her blood. Curtis sat in shock as he witnessed the whole scene unfold before his own eyes from his car. As he heard the sirens begin and suddenly remembered that the police station was only a few blocks away, his first impulse was just to drive off, but he saw Joose as a little brother he had taken under his wing. He felt somewhat responsible for him, and he had way more love for him than just to leave him that way.

Curtis reluctantly got out of his car and ran over to Joose; he grabbed him up from behind and underneath his arms as he spoke near his ear, "Come on homie, I know, I know, this is hard... But the Cops are comin' we gotta go!" Joose looked into Curtis' face while still caught up in his daze, wanting more than anything for this to be some horrible nightmare that he would awake from any minute. "I killed her, Curt; I killed my own Mama." Curtis continued to drag his friend to the car without responding. After he had Joose seated in the passenger seat, he ran back and quickly grabbed the bag of money and the gun, returned, and jumped into his driver's seat, pulling away from the curb with a loud squeal of his tires on the street.

Chapter 6

"65th Street! 65th Street!" The bus driver loudly yelled over the speakers as Joose jerked forward, opening his eyes and realizing that he must have dozed off for a minute. His exit was coming up next; he gazed out the window at the familiar surroundings of his Grandmother's neighborhood. He knew his Grandparents would be eager to hear how his interview had gone. He dreaded having to tell them that he knew he didn't get the job, but he would have to do just that. After his mother's untimely death, that was where he and his brother had been sent off to live. The circumstances surrounding the death of Anita Phillips were kept a secret between Joose and Curtis. On that day, during the ride home, Curtis looked at Joose with tears in his eyes and swore to him that he would never tell a soul what had happened that day. He also advised Joose to do the same. Joose had spent the rest of his life after that day in an unending guilt-ridden torment that never gave him peace. He always had nightmares and flashbacks of the day when he had killed his mother.

Once again, as he had done so many times before, he silently asked God to forgive him for what he had done and to help him change his life. He exited the bus and decided to stop at the Food Mart on the corner to pick up a few groceries. He thought at least he could try to contribute to his Grandparent's household this time to show them how he was changing. His thoughts rested on his younger brother Terrance for a minute. Terrance had always been the better of the two of them. Terrance stayed in school and got excellent grades. Terrance had always silently observed Joose going down the wrong path but, within himself, had made up his mind that he owed their mother more than that. He did so well in high school that he was awarded an academic scholarship. He now attends Montclair State University in pursuit of becoming a physician. His Grandparents were good people and truly meant well, but Joose had finished his adolescence growing up in the shadow of his younger brother and being constantly compared to him by his Grandparents and the rest of his family. He loved his brother with all of his heart, but he was more than aware of the small amount of jealousy he carried because he had not been smart enough to take the road his brother had traveled to become a success the legal way. Joose pushed all of these negative thoughts out of his mind so that he could focus on the best way to budget the 20-dollar bill that he would be spending in the Food Mart today. He passed the dairy aisle and picked up some eggs, milk, and a pack of cheese. He went on to the deli section and bought some ham and salami. He looked around at the other families in the store shopping and briefly thought of how good it would be not to be restricted to such a small budget. As he finished shopping and headed to the front counter, he tried to remember if he had forgotten anything important.

   Just as he was beginning to step in line behind a woman with a cart full of groceries, the service light on the next aisle lit up, and the Checker announced, "Next, please." Joose hurriedly stepped in the next line as he saw from the side of his eye that someone else was quickly walking toward the opening. "Good Afternoon." The Checker nonchalantly greeted Joose. Without answering, Joose began to load his groceries onto the checkstand. He looked into the face of the cashier and then did a double take. There was something familiar about the cashier. He strained to read her name tag, which held the title Assistant Manager and, right below that, Iesha Turner. Joose smiled and said out loud, "No, I didn't just run into my little cousin!"

The cashier looked at Joose, startled at first, then her expression turned into amusement as she smiled and cocked her head to one side. "Joose...is that you?" "Yeah, it's me, girl, look at you I aint seen you in years!!" Iesha stepped from around the counter and warmly embraced her cousin; she knew the last time she had heard anything about him, he was in prison. It was no secret throughout the family that he was a Jailbird- always in and out. "How are you doing, Joo? Staying out of trouble, I hope!" She added teasingly. Joose eyed his cousin for a minute, looking at her jewelry and her stylish dark blue denim Levi jeans and silk Louis Vuitton top. He noticed how she had the matching Louis Vuitton belt and watch to accessorize with the top, not to mention the matching boots, which he noticed when she stepped from behind the counter.

"Man, Cuzz, I'm just trying to make it. I'm fresh out, and I'm trying to do right this time around. I been spending a lot of time in prayer, and I feel like God is gonna help me make it right this time." Iesha nodded in understanding as she continued to scan his items. She felt a little reluctant to show her cousin any real love because the Joose that she knew was low down and dirty. She honestly felt within herself that he probably had not changed that much. "Give me your number, cousin; I'm gonna hit you up!" Joose said to Iesha, he ignored the vibe that he felt coming from her that let him know she did not want to offer her number and truly preferred their little reunion to end right there in the grocery store. "I..I don't even have a pen." Iesha lied, hoping her cousin would take the hint, but Joose did the opposite. He began to dig around in his pockets until he came out with a pen and a small piece of paper. "There we go!" Joose said, smiling. Inside his mind, he was already planning on calling Iesha and asking her to hook him up at her job and possibly to see if she had any Christian girlfriends he could hook up with cause a brother was lonely. Iesha quickly scribbled down her cell phone number and handed it to Joose. "The weekends are the best time to catch me; I'm always working these days," Iesha said while emphasizing the last part of her statement. Joose caught it all, but he dismissed it because he knew he would surely have a small piece of his cousins' success. He left the Food Mart with a wide grin spread across his face, as he silently thanked God that he had run into Iesha, and now he felt certain that things would change in his favor soon.

Joose strolled down the street with the bag of groceries in his arms, whistling a tune that reminded him of old times. As he neared his grandparents' home, he saw his brother's car parked in the driveway. He was halfway hoping that Terrance would not be home when he got there because he didn't want to announce that he didn't get the job in front of him. Joose slowly approached the front door and turned his key into the lock. "Joose, That you?" His Grandpa Jo-Jo cried from the living room. "Yeah, it's me, Pop. I brought some groceries." "Oh, good, son. Bless your soul." Jo-Jo stated as he slowly crept into the kitchen from the living room. "Where's GG?" Joose asked, hoping that he could have a private word with his grandma. "I'm right here, Joo!" GG shouted from behind him, "Give me my sugar boy!" She commanded, extending her arms for him to hug her. Joose smiled and gave his grandmother a tight embrace. He was so relieved that she didn't ask about his interview right away. He wanted to forget about how things had gone for the time being.

Joose stood silently for a second admiring his grandmother; at Eighty-seven years old, she still looked no older than fifty. She had suffered many years of loneliness after Joose's natural Grandfather, Henry, died while they were both still young. After many years of refusing to go on without him, she finally agreed to do as the rest of her family urged and advised her to do; she moved on but only under one condition; GG made it plain and clear that although she may marry again she will always be Georgia Turner, and she would keep her first husband's last name because it was a part of her legacy she felt. Joose lightly shook his head to snatch himself from his thoughts, "Look, GG, I got some groceries for us." "I see... well, now, what do we have here?" GG asked with a smile on her face as she looked down at Joose over her reading glasses; she began reaching into the bag, pulling out the food items one by one, and commenting on the smart selections that Joose had made at the store. Terrance walked in and nodded at Joose, "Wasup, big bro!" He raised his arm to grab Joose's hand, shake it, and embrace like they always did. Joose looked around at Terrance with a look of disgust and hurt stricken in his eyes. He tried to mask it as he half smiled, "Hey Terrance, wasup man?" The two embraced, but not before Terrance took note of the look in his brothers' face. He was aware of the envy that his older brother had toward him and the two different roads that life had taken them both down, but regardless of that, Terrance still held his brother in the highest respect and looked up to him. After all, they needed to be there for each other now that their mother was gone. Terrance began to look into the refrigerator, and as he grabbed the pitcher of

Kool-Aid, he asked, "So how did the interview go, Joo?" Joose silently mumbled a curse word under his breath as Terrance, GG, and Pop looked in his direction, anxiously awaiting his response.

Joose stood for a moment in silence as he looked back into the faces of each of them; nothing was harder for him than admitting that he was a failure. Without saying anything, he turned and stormed out of the kitchen, on through the living room, and out of the back door, slamming it shut behind him. He yelled out as he blindly swung into the air, fighting an unseen enemy. He was so frustrated, he had been holding it all in, trying to stay positive but now it felt like more than he could bear. He swung his fists into the air one after the other, literally fighting the wind. He didn't know why he was doing this, but at the moment, it helped release his frustration. Tears burned beneath his eyelids and finally spilled out from the corners of his eyes and streamed down his face uncontrolled; feeling overly exhausted, he crumbled down on the grass beneath him and hung his head between his shoulders as he cried at first silently as the pain burned from deep within his chest, then louder and louder until his cries were heart-wrenching, unrestrained sobs that released all of his life's aches and pains.

By this time, his grandparents were watching him from the living room window, wishing that they could comfort his pain but knowing that it was best that he be left alone for the time being. Joose sobbed until he felt that all the tears had dried up. He lay back on the grass, his soul feeling tired as he stared up into the blue sky. He silently asked God, "Why?" Why the reason for this life he was living? Why did he get corrupted so young? Why did his father leave him alone at such a young age to face a heartless world? Why?

Sometimes, he felt like killing himself to be rid of the heartache, but he knew that he couldn't just die and leave Terrance alone. Still, sometimes, the pain and the guilt were way too much to deal with. Deep in his heart, he felt that God did not hear his cries, and he felt alone. He knew that the bible said all he had to do was ask, and he would instantly be forgiven, but sometimes he just did not believe it. He lay there for a while longer, watching the birds fly across the sky in their groups, forming patterns and floating so freely in the wind. At that moment, Joose prayed, "God, Please listen to me. One day, I wanna be free like one of those birds in the air. I want you to remove this pain from my heart. I want you to bless my life and make it better. If you love me, Lord, Please show me that you can hear me?"

Joose continued to stare into the sky, and out of the corner of his eye, he saw a movement; as he turned his head to the side, he saw a big, beautiful butterfly with many different colors in it, lightly bouncing on its wings and seemingly fluttering straight toward him. Joose's eyes widened in amazement as he watched the butterfly. He felt a tingle run along the surface of his skin as he realized God was answering his prayer and proving that he had been heard. The beautiful butterfly landed on a sunflower less than a foot from his face and sat there while Joose gazed at it in admiration. As the butterfly turned and fluttered its beautiful wings to fly away, Joose heard a voice from within the depths of his spirit. "See, I do love you, and I always hear you when you call on me. Your life will get better, my son."

Joose sat there marveling as he clung to the voice from within him, too real to be imagined. He knew that he had just heard the voice of The Lord. He began to smile as he realized that he was not alone and special enough for the Lord to speak to him. Joose continued to lie in that spot, mesmerized by the peacefulness that had now consumed his soul. He lay there until the sun began to set, went inside the house to his bedroom, turned out the lights, and fell asleep.

At the end of Iesha's shift that evening, she got into her car and turned down the CD that was at full blast from earlier. When she was feeling good, she enjoyed nothing more than blasting her music and riding down the street with all the windows down, the air flowing through the car, and stares from people on the street looking at her flashy money-green 1998 Mercedes Benz. However, this evening, she did not feel good. She had an attitude the rest of the day after she ran into Joose. She wished that she had just told him that she did not want him calling her and that she could do nothing for him. As she thought about him after he had left the store earlier, she was sure he would probably call her to borrow money or even beg to stay at her house if grandma and them got tired of his sorry jailbird behind. Coming in contact with him had completely ruined what would have been a great day. Iesha had received several calls from a few of her guy friends as well as her sister that day, but each time the phone rang she felt a sick anticipation of the call being from Joose and was reluctant to answer.

She found that she could not stop thinking about it, no matter how hard she tried. She felt within herself that she had worked very hard to get where she was now, and if she had to work hard, then so did everybody else. She made it up in her mind that she would just avoid Joose for as long as possible. She didn't owe him anything, she told herself. After all, they weren't even close. Sometimes, as kids, when her mom would take them to visit Aunty Nita, Joose wouldn't even offer to share any snacks or other types of treats they had in their house, Iesha remembered. She shook her head and spoke out loud, "Please don't call me; I ain't got nothin' for you....at all!" At that, she turned up her music and began to bob her head to the beat as she decided that she would not help him.

A few days passed before she got the first phone call; it was from a number she didn't recognize, so she let the voicemail pick up, "Yeah... I'm not available...either that, or I don't wanna talk to you. Leave a message at the tone, and I might call you back...Laytahhh!" Joose held the phone for a second before speaking, "Hey, wasup girl! I see you got it goin' on from every level, go on wit' yo bad self! Ha, ha, ha, ha, ha, anyhow, girl, this is your C-Lowousin Joose, call me back when you get my message, it's real important I need to holla at you...Hit me up!"

Joose hung up the phone and silently prayed that Iesha would return his call in a timely manner. When Iesha heard the message, she started calling him back but decided to wait and carefully plan her response first. She tried to think of different ways to tell him she could not help him. Then she realized she had not even given her cousin the benefit of the doubt. What if he wasn't even calling her for help? What if he really just needed someone to talk to who would put some positive words in his ear? If that were the case, she thought the least she could do was talk to the man. Iesha turned this over in her mind for a few days, and then she decided to consult her mother for advice.

After work had ended that Friday evening, Iesha went to her mom's house. She knocked loudly, and Tish came to the door. "Hey, Girl, what brings you bye?" Her older sister greeted her as she grabbed her and hugged her warmly. "Oh, nothin' much, just wanted to talk to momma for a minute; what you up to?" She asked Tish. "Girl, studying hard as usual...I got midterms comin' up on Monday, girl, you know what that's like." Iesha shook her head and smiled, "Girl, tell me about it, mines are right around the corner, but you already know, 'we gotta do what we gotta do to get where we need to be!'" Tish had joined in the last part of the saying that she and her sister always quoted to each other; they both ended in unison and began laughing as they slapped a high five.

Shielah entered the living room then, "Well, well, if it ain't my lil' Miss Iesha. Girl, it feel like you livin' outta state or something you stay away so much! Get ova' here and gimme' my suga!" Iesha ran to hug her mother, and the two held each other tightly while Shielah smothered her daughter with kisses on her forehead and cheeks. "Uhhmmm, Uhmmmm it's good to see you chile, what you been up to beside work and school?" Iesha sat on the couch as her mother sat in her favorite chair beside her before responding. "Actually, nothin' really besides work and school; you won't guess who came into the Food Mart last week." By this time, Tish had taken a break from her studies and had joined her mother and sister in the living room. She was sitting on the loveseat next to the couch, her feet curled up underneath her, intently listening to the conversation. "Who?" Shielah asked. "Joose...He just got out!" "Whaaaaat!" Both Sheilah and Tish shrieked at the same time. Tish shook her head from side to side, "Lord have mercy on that boy; I wonder if he's had enough this time around...What was he doin' tryin' to steal? You know he aint got no money."

Sheilah seemed lost in thought as she gazed down at the floor; Iesha responded dryly, "He was buying some groceries. Evidently, he done got some money from somewhere. He just so happened to come to my checkout line of all places and recognized me before I recognized him. He begged for my number, and you know I didn't want to give it." All three of the women sat in silence for a few seconds. Iesha looked at her mother, "Ma, that's part of the reason why I came over...I need some advice." Sheilah looked her daughter in the eyes for a full minute before responding, which caused Iesha to shift to her seat. She knew her mother all too well and knew that when it took her a while to answer, it was a well-thought-out response. "Well baby, I know that you are your own woman now; and I trust always that I raised you the right way despite the challenges we all faced, God brought us through. Honey, I must say that we all get down on our luck sometimes. Your cousin has gone through a great deal in his life, he lost his mother and my sister when he was only 13 years old. So I have a deep soft spot in my heart for Joose...I feel that if God has blessed you to be in a position to help your cousin out, you should help him in any way that you can."

Iesha looked back at her mother for a second, then rolled her eyes to the floor. "I was hoping you wouldn't tell me that momma." Sheilah thought a few more seconds before speaking again, "I know that it may seem inconvenient for your cousin to call on you, but everything happens for a reason, Iesha; God may be trying to test your heart. Remember, Chile, what goes around comes around, and you always reap what you sow... that's why it's always best to sow goodness and righteousness because it will always come back to you."

Iesha looked over at her sister, "What you thank about all this, Tish? He done already called me leavin a message the other day talkin' bout, 'call him back, it's important' I aint called him yet cause I don't know what to say." Tish gazed back at Iesha, then looked over at her mother, who had a smirk on her face, ready to jump down her throat if she had given the wrong advice. "Girl, I would just pray on it...and be careful. I wouldn't say don't consider helpin' him, but just make sure that he has changed from how he used to be and he ain't tryin to use you." Iesha looked back to her mother, who nodded approvingly to Tish's advice. She nodded her head as she looked back and forth from her mother to her sister, "Yeah, you right, that's exactly what I'm gon' do...Pray on it." Iesha ate some of her mother's home cooking that she had prepared for dinner that night before she left to come home to her cozy but empty apartment. As she did her normal routine of showering before bed, she was grateful that she could sleep in for a little while tomorrow morning, then go to her classes at the college, which began at 10:30, and from there to her manicurist to get a fill and another pedicure. She smoothed her body butter onto her naked flesh and crawled into bed after turning off the lights. She lay there and thought about the words from her mother and the advice from her sister, "You always reap what you sow'...'Just pray on it'...' What goes around comes around'...' Everybody falls down on their luck sometimes'..." The words swirled around in her mind actively before she fell asleep.

Chapter 7

That night, Iesha's dreams haunted her. She saw her cousin Joose begging and pursuing her for help, and she avoided him, dodging him, and went through extreme measures so as not to have any contact with him. She even saw Joose looking homeless and hungry in her dream, and he was attempting to get help from her, but in the dream, she turned her back on him. Then her dream switched scenarios, and she saw herself dressed raggedy and dirty, sitting on the side of a curb, holding a tin can out to strangers passing by and hoping for a handout. In the dream, her now beautiful and glowing mane was a dirty mangle of nappy strands that resembled dusty dreadlocks. Her face was dirty, and she looked poor beyond all imagination. She could vividly smell the putrid odor coming from her own body, the result of days if not weeks with no bath or shower, as well as feel the pain of intense hunger emitting from her belly. As she watched this scenario unfolding from an unseen place in her dream, she felt pain welling inside of her chest as she watched this homeless and unfortunate version of herself being humiliated, from begging with people passing by and scoffing, laughing, or just ignoring her altogether. In the dream, she began to cry, and at that, she awoke to find that she really had tears in her eyes.

Iesha jerked herself awake and opened her eyes, then sat up in bed. She was sweat-drenched and breathing heavily like she had just run a mile. The dream she had just experienced was so vivid that it horrified her. She still had tears streaming down her face as she felt all of the emotions and recalled the terrible details of how she looked, smelled, and felt. She had never experienced anything like this before. As she sat in bed upright, she pulled her knees up to her chest and hugged her legs; she rocked back and forth, still crying. She was now attempting to reason with herself that it must have just been a silly dream related to the things her mom told her the night before. She slowly began to let her tears subside; looking over at the alarm clock on the nightstand, she noted that it was 4:30 am. A brief thought crossed her mind that she should at least return Joose's call today. She lay back on the bed and let the remnants of the dream fade from her mind.

She began to speak to herself out loud, "Girl, you gotta stop trippin'. You know you are too much of a diva to end up in that position; it was just a bad dream; people do have those. Besides, you gotta do what you gotta do; Momma and them can give all kinds of advice, but in the end, they sho' ain't handin' out no help!" Iesha chuckled to herself as she wiped the last of her tears away. Iesha continued, "Shoot, he is a full-grown man. If I can help and it won't inconvenience me, I will, but if not, oh well." At that, she turned over and went back to sleep; this time, she did not dream at all.

The next day, nothing uneventful happened; Iesha kept finding reasons not to call Joose back. Deep down, she hoped that he did not call her again, and he didn't. Early Sunday morning, Iesha woke up and got ready for church. It was her weekly tradition to go to The Holy Temple Baptist Church. Now that the years had passed, her mother and sister regularly attended again. Sometimes, her brothers Dante and Damion would even decide to come out for fellowship, even though they now lived way down in Jersey City in their shared bachelor pad two-bedroom townhouse.

Iesha stood at the bathroom mirror and arranged her hair with a pretty yellow flower clip, pulling it to the side. She was wearing a beautiful yellow blazer and skirt set. Her silk top underneath was blended with an array of sensuous colors, such as soft pinks, yellows, and blues, along with pastel greens. She was setting it off with her pastel green high heels with the strap wrapped around her ankle. As Iesha began to apply her lip gloss and fill in her eyebrows, she smiled to herself as she thought about how good it would be to see her brothers, and she hoped they would be at church this morning. She was proud of both of them. Dante' was going to construction school to become a foreman, a profitable trade that would eventually yield him a well-off lifestyle. Damion was pursuing a modeling career. He spent ample time traveling out of state, meeting with agents doing photo shoots, and building his portfolio. He had already been featured in a local magazine modeling a new urban hip-hop style of men's clothing, and he received a lot of recognition because of it.

Sheilah was so proud of all her children and counted them all successful in her eyes. Iesha finished up in the bathroom and made her way to the kitchen. She put a slice of bread in the toaster and poured herself a glass of orange juice. She was just about to take a sip when her cell phone rang; she ran across the room to pick it up and was just about to answer before recognizing that it was Joose calling. She held the phone for a moment, trying to make a split-second decision on what to do; she finally decided to answer. This would be the first time she had spoken with her cousin since she saw him at the Food Mart over a week ago. She took a deep breath then answered, trying to sound surprised, "Hello?... Oh hey, wasup, Joose!" She smiled, attempting to make it sound like she was happy to hear from him. She silently prayed that he would not ask her for anything. "Hey, Iesha, girl, you sure are hard to get a hold of...what have you been up to?" Joose asked, trying to feel her out. "Uhhm, I told you I be workin' a lot cousin, I have two different jobs so they consume most of my time. Usually, when I finally get home each day, I'm so tired I just crash. What have you been up to?" Joose paused for a second before answering, "Well, just like you have been busy working, I have been busy lookin' for work; man, it sho' is rough out here to find a job. I been applyin' everywhere too." Joose ended his last sentence with silence to give his cousin a chance to respond. "Yeah, I hear ya; it is real rough out here." Iesha agreed. When Joose saw that she was not going to offer any help, he decided to just go for it, "Well cousin, that is part of why I am calling; I really need your help. I noticed that you are the assistant manager at the Food Mart. Could you hook me up? Man, I would really appreciate it; I will take anything I can get right now." Iesha did not respond immediately; as she rolled her eyes to the ceiling, she tried to choose her words carefully. She pondered for a moment because she prided herself on being honest, but she did not want to hurt her cousin or be cold-hearted, although she could not deny that she just did not want to help him. "Look, Joose, I know you need help, but I can't promise anything. I have busted my butt to get where I am now in the Food Mart, and it wasn't easy. I really don't feel all that confident in hookin' you up with the way you be goin' back and forth to jail. I just gotta be real!" Iesha stated flatly as she rolled her eyes and held her finger in the air. Joose was obviously a little insulted when he responded,

"Iesha, I feel you on that, but I gave my heart to God this last time I was locked up, and I am trying so hard to do the right thing.....I promised The Lord that I would stay outta' trouble. No more sellin' dope, no more robbin' folks, no more pimpin', no more trying to cheat my way through life! I'm serious about tryin' to do right this time around, no matter what it takes. Please help me, little cousin?" Joose was on the other end of the phone with his hands stretched before him, begging his younger cousin to help him out.

He felt humiliated because although he was used to living a criminal lifestyle, he was used to living lavishly. The previous times that he had been released from prison, he never stayed broke for long. The whole family knew that Joose was used to driving the newest cars and having the nicest plush furniture in his apartments. Females were known to fight and compete with each other for his time and attention. He was known for having two to three or more sluts and hood rats all at the same time, who all knew about each other and prided themselves that they could claim to be with Bloody Joose from G.P.M.

He held a hood status that was not easily attained from his years of putting in violent and dangerous work for the Garden Mafia. He was still respected and feared by his other gangster family members, and he was idolized and looked up to by the younger gangsters like some kind of legend. The roughest part of it all for him was the fact that at the drop of a hat, he could have it all back and then some. All he would have to do was pay a visit to Doctor Willy and Dirty Black, who still ran the Garden Projects Mafia, and although now they were both well into their 50s, they were still in the business of recruiting young gangsters.

Each time he had been released from jail or prison in the past, he would make the projects his first stop; he was always embraced with the same love and acceptance that had come from day one. Doctor Willy would hug him, bring him into his apartment, and sit him down as Black would begin rolling up the blunt for them to all smoke and get high on. They would all talk and laugh, with Dr and Black filling Joose in on all the events of the hood that he had missed out on while he was gone. Usually, Black would have a wide grin spread across his face as he related something like, "Yeah, Joo, Nigga you missed it! That fool Chocolate smoked Lil' Drew in wide open daylight in front of everybody! He crazy..He didn't even care; you know Michelle is out there hoeing again..she all out there man, and Big Shirl done got them kids took again, she ain't gon get' em back this time watch!" Usually, the talk would go on for an hour or so, with the two reacquainting him and getting him caught up on hood gossip. Then, they would handle the business. Doctor would always give Joose anywhere from Ten to Twenty thousand dollars and a Kilogram of Cocaine. He would smile and tell him, "Alright, you know how we do it. Just bring back my share and my interest this time next week...after that, you'll be alright." He would also give Joose a list of phone numbers. Usually, the females were prostitutes who were eager to work for him, selling their bodies and selling his drugs for him, and the males on the list were young thugs who were ready to sell his drugs, kill anyone that seemed to be some sort of threat, or even perform high maintenance robberies on banks, and high-end jewelry stores. Within one week, Joose would be high-rolling again and right back to his cold-hearted ways, but none less- supporting himself.

    He now sat silently on the opposite end of the phone, awaiting Iesha's response; she held the phone in blank silence for a while. Joose found himself wondering if she were still there, "Hello..." He asked, "Yes, I'm still here, Joo, you gon' have to give me some time to see what I can do; I will have to try and pull some strings with your criminal background and all....." She purposely emphasized the last statement, knowing it would sound cruel but not caring at the moment. "And please don't keep calling me about it; I will call you and let you know....Okay?" Iesha said with a smirk on her face, blatantly revealing that she did not want to assist him. Joose heard all of the sarcasm in Iesha's voice, which bothered him. He wished he could tell her to go to hell and that he didn't need her help, but he knew the opposite was true. He had to use this new opportunity as a possible stepping stone. "Alright, cousin...." He said with a smile, "I really appreciate it here." "Um, hummm. Okay, talk to you later." Iesha quickly replied, hanging up the phone. She stood there for a second, shaking her head. After she hung up the phone and realized that her toast had popped up, she grabbed it from the toaster, hurriedly spread some peach preserves on it, and chewed it vigorously while thinking over her conversation with Joose. After she finished her toast, she drank her juice and grabbed her purse as she headed out the door.

She pulled into the already crowded church parking lot and waived at a few of the regular church brothers and sisters as she navigated her freshly washed and waxed Benz into one of the nearby spots. Before she exited the car, she silently prayed, "God, please help me do the right thing...I don't know what to do concerning my cousin; you know, Lord, that I have built a good reputation for myself out of all my hard work. I don't even wanna' bring Joose on the scene because people will be looking at him and judging me for his actions. Lord, Please forgive me if I am being wrong, but you know every time he comes home, he is hollerin' that he gave his life to you, and before you know, he is right back at it." She took a deep breath before continuing, "God, please make another way for Joose besides me having to help him; I just don't want him workin' alongside me, Please?" Deep down, Iesha felt a little guilty for praying what she knew was a selfish prayer, but she did not know what else to do. She now honestly felt within herself that all would be well because she knew that God always heard her and that he would open another door for her cousin due to her prayer. Iesha resulted within herself at that point that she would not have to help Joose because God would make another way for him. She shrugged her shoulders as she got out of the car and began walking toward the front of the church. "All is well..." She said to herself.

When she walked inside the church, she was surprised to see that her mother and Tish were already sitting in the front row on the left-hand side. Usually, she beat them here every Sunday, but what surprised her more was that her two brothers were on the side of her mother. Iesha's face spread into a big smile as she put her hands to her mouth and stepped up to the front row with the rest of her family. The rest of her family stood up and hugged for a moment before she sat between Dante' and her mother.

The praise and worship were already in full swing as the choir emotionally belted out a strong and mighty version of "Praise is What I Do." The choir's best male singer, Brother Malcolm, was now in the front of the congregation, almost on his knees, holding the microphone in one hand while the other was up stretched toward heaven as he had tears in the corners of his eyes, "Oh the devil can't stand your praise. He hates your praise. Praise is what I do." Malcolm was singing so passionately that almost the whole churchhouse was on their feet, praising in agreement. Iesha realized that she arrived just in time as she stood to her feet shouting, "Hallelujah!! Glory to God! Yes, Lord, have your way, Jesus! Yes!" She was waving an arm in the air toward the Lord with her eyes closed. Her mother and Tish were on their feet and giving praise.

When the choir ended, the pastor came up to the podium, raised his arms in the air, and the congregation continued to yell out praises. After a few moments, the room slowly began to get quiet so the pastor could speak. Pastor Brown allowed his gaze to scan the church before he spoke. He was an older man who had pastored this church for over forty years. His family was of well report, and he had never done anything to cause a scandal in the community in all his years. He was well respected and loved by the entire community. He cleared his throat before speaking, "Praise the Lord Saints, let's open in prayer. Father God, thank you for the opportunity to be gathered in your holy name yet another day, Father; we love you and can't live without you. Please bless the word going forth today, bless the hearers, bless our families and those we don't know Father God, in Jesus' name...Amen." "Amen," the Church said in agreement.

"Let's start out today by welcoming our first-time attendees," Pastor Brown continued. This was a little different because there were usually no first-time attendees; every one that attended Holy Temple was regular. A few members began looking around to see who was new when the pastor said, "If this is your first time fellowshipping with us, please stand to your feet and introduce yourself?" At first, there was no movement, but a tall young man in the very last row of the church stood in a dark blue suit.

Iesha turned to look and was shocked to see Joose standing in the visitor's place. Her mouth dropped open as he opened his mouth to speak, "Hello, my name is Juwan, and I recently gave my life to Terrancet; I am just lookin' for somewhere to fellowship." Everyone began clapping and nodding in approval; as Shielah recognized her nephew's face, she stood to her feet and spoke out loud, "Joose, is that you, baby....it's me, your Aunty Sheilah!" She stretched her arms out as Joose stepped out from the back row and ran to her embrace. Tish, Dante', and Damion all stood to their feet to welcome their cousin, but Iesha just sat there with a half smile. The pastor began to speak as the mini-reunion was going forth, "Praise be to God's son, you are at home with us...welcome, welcome, welcome!" He smiled as he spoke into the microphone looking at Joose.

Joose now had tears in his eyes as he felt a new type of acceptance. He had never felt any real love from anyone but his parents when they were alive, his gang family, and his grandparents. But now, he was feeling something like love and the new realization that he had a real fresh chance to do right. He felt right at home instantly. He looked over at Iesha as he hugged Tish and waved at her. She grinned and waved back. Although Iesha was smiling, she did not feel very happy in her heart, even as she watched the emotional scene unfold; down deep inside, she looked at Joose and wondered if maybe he was even faking this. Suddenly, she could not wait for the service to be over; Joose sat next to Sheilah and enjoyed the rest of the service.

After Church, Iesha ended up going home. To her family's surprise, she did not stay to have Sunday dinner at her mother's house. Her mind felt heavy with the expectation that Joose was putting on her. She tried as best as she could to put it out of her mind, but no matter what, she just could not help it. She needed to make a decision. She decided that night that she would try to mention the scenario to the lead manager the next day at work and see what the response would be, and then she would be able to make a more informed decision.

Meanwhile, Joose was at Sheilah's house having the best day he could remember in a long time. Sheilah prepared a Sunday dinner of chicken and dumplings, rice, honey-cured ham, Collard Greens, and cornbread. While she was in the kitchen preparing dinner, Joose sat with his cousins in the cozy living room, reminiscing on old times. He felt so good as he sat back and relished the warm feeling he felt when being with other family members besides Terrance, G.G, and Pop.

He looked around at the old pictures that covered the walls and decorated the stands in the home of Iesha, Tish, Damion, and Dante' when they were children. He even admired the old pictures of his aunty when she was younger. He stood to his feet as he walked over to the walls to get a better look at some of the pictures. He nearly froze in place, and he felt his heart skip a beat as his eyes met with the sad-looking eyes of a beautiful young woman in her early twenties holding a baby; he recognized her to be his beloved mother. This was the picture that she had taken the day she was released from the hospital after giving birth to him. Joose now studied the picture that he had only seen once or twice before in his whole life, and he allowed his eyes to drink in every detail of the old photograph. Her beautiful silky jet-black hair, sweet almond-shaped eyes, and half smile almost masked the pain that she must have still felt from forcing out the 10-pound baby boy that she now clutched in her arms. Although the picture was in black and white, Joose vividly saw his mother's smooth cocoa-colored complexion and snow-white teeth, barely revealed in this photograph. A feeling of deep guilt began to rise in him again as he wondered within himself if Anita would have still died so young had she never had him.

He felt the tears beginning to well up inside of him as he tried with all his might to fight them from coming to the surface. Just then, Sheilah, emerging from the kitchen and wiping her hands on her apron heading toward the back of the house, stopped in her tracks when she noticed that Joose was staring at the picture of his mother. She stood a few minutes in silence, watching him as he stared at the picture. When she noticed the pain on his face, she quietly walked up behind him and placed a soft hand on his shoulder, which caused him to jump a little, being jerked from his thoughts. "You know, this was always my favorite picture of yo' mama. "Sheilah softly said, "On that day, she was so proud to have a healthy baby boy." At those words, a few tears ran from Joose's eyes and hurriedly raced down to his chin, dropping on his suit jacket. "Your daddy snapped that picture as soon as she stepped out of the hospital doors before she got into the car. When she got home we were all waiting to surprise her, bless her heart...she was so, so happy." Sheilah gently grabbed Joose's shoulders as she steered him toward her; she looked inside his face, which was full of hurt, "Honey, I know you miss her, but just know that she is still with you in spirit...only her shell is gone, that's it!" She hugged and held him close to her, which warmed his heart. "Dinner will be ready soon, okay, Baby? You go get your hands washed so you can eat a good Sunday meal with your family, okay?" Joose nodded, "Okay, Aunty......thank you for being here for me." Sheilah hugged him again and began to walk on through the hallway. Joose ate dinner with his cousins and laughed some more; afterward, his cousin Dante' dropped him off at G.G.'s house.

Joose truly felt like things were changing in his favor. He was so happy that he had gone to church, and he felt things would be different this time. He went to his room, laid out his bedclothes, and then took a hot shower. As the water ran over his face, he visualized that it was also washing away the hurts and pains of the day. He closed his eyes and vividly saw again the picture of his mother from earlier. He began to speak out loud, "Momma, I'm so, so, sorry. I would do anything to have you back, even trade places with you if I could. I'm so sorry, Momma; please forgive me." He tried to push the memories from his mind of that horrible day and the last time he had seen her alive, but once again, he found himself reliving that old nightmare. When he finally snatched himself from his thoughts, he realized he must have been in the shower for quite some time because the water was no longer hot but lukewarm.

Joose exited the shower and went to his room, where he dried off and put on his bedclothes. He got under the warm blankets of the full-sized bed and turned off the bedside lamp. As he lay there, he had visions of his future, as he had dreamed it would be. He saw himself in a nice three-piece suit, carrying a briefcase, heading to work for some sort of successful company. He saw his family as a beautiful daughter and handsome son with a beautiful wife who upheld him through life's trials and tribulations. Joose clearly saw a big yellow home by the ocean shore, bright green grass, and newly parked cars for him and his wife. These thoughts gave him a sense of peace and well-being as he allowed the visions to rock him to sleep. Yes, the future would be better than the past; his last thought before his sleep consumed him.

Chapter 8

"Hurry up! You betta get up here! Else I'm gon leave you!" The dirty couple made their way up the street to the Food Mart. They were following their normal ritual of going into the store at 3 p.m. as the shift change was taking place. Jackie had been homeless for four long years now. Ever since she got wrapped up with her boyfriend, C-Low, her entire life had immediately spiraled downhill.

As she hurried in behind C-Low, her bare feet burning through the holes in her old worn-out tennis shoes from the 105-degree heat of that Friday, August afternoon, she reminisced about how her life was before C-Low. She was a supervisor for the Transportation Department in the State of Colorado's downtown office. She held a very high position in the State office; many people looked up to her. She had worked her way up quickly from graduating from College at the top of her class with a Master's Degree. She had purposely forgotten the poverty in which she was born into because it left a bitter taste in her mouth, so as soon as she was in a position to do so within her new 200,000.00 dollar a year career, she purchased one of the most lavish homes she could find, as well as bought herself a brand new Lexus. She prepaid a butler/maid cleaning service for a whole year.

It felt so good to spoil herself and live the good life for once; she felt so powerful and rich. She enjoyed the attention she received every time she drove her new Baby Pink Cotton Candy colored Lexus luxury sports car. And when she walked in to sit at her desk within her beautiful plushed-out office, she would hear hushed whispers as her staff hastened to look busy just because she was passing by. She also enjoyed being strict with her employees, who took their orders from her. She felt like the position that she had held would last forever; she hardly had to do any work, and all she had to do was order the other employees on what documents to file and what provisions to make. Her secretary handled her phone calls, typed all her memos, and arranged all her meetings. Most of the time, she had to figure out what stylish business suit she would wear daily, and that was the best part. She looked the part so well. Jackie Whitman, she was a young, sexy, black mainstream professional, and it felt damn good.

It seemed she could hear them now, "Ms.Whitman, may I please have two more days on my report? It will be in, I promise." Or, "Ms. Whitman, Do you like how I organized our new filing system? I did it just for you!" "Ms. Whitman. Ms. Whitman." "Ms. Whitman! Hurry yo' slow ass up! We almost there, messin' wit' you we aint gon' have no dam grub tonight!" The voice of C-Low rang out, breaking into her thoughts; her heart sank deep in her chest as she realized that even daydreaming and reminiscing had become only a couple of the many luxuries that she could no longer afford.

They reached the front of the store at about a quarter to three. They both knew that the young black assistant manager would be pulling up in her shiny green Benz any second. The routine always went successful for them; once Iesha got in and put her things away, she would have a brief discussion with the check stand cashier who would be leaving for the day, and then they would count out the money and take some of it to the back to deposit into the bank the next day. Usually, that kept them so busy that the dirty couple would slip into the store, hit up the deli section, grab turkey, ham, and salami lunch meats and cheeses, then the bread isle, and last but not least, they would go to the beverage section where they would each grab two to four sodas a piece. If they were lucky, they also could snatch a few candy bars a piece. The whole 'shopping spree', as the couple usually called it, only lasted about 5 minutes. They would slip in unnoticed and slip back out unnoticed.

    Today, things went a little differently than usual. When the assistant manager arrived, she headed straight to the back instead of going to the check stand as usual. The couple looked at each other; Jackie spoke first, "I don't know, C-Low...maybe we should wait a few minutes...they might see us if she aint doin' the switch when we walk in." C-Low looked at Jackie, then twisted his mouth, "No, we aint gon' wait...we gon' go up in there and handle our business, now get to steppin'!" The two walked into the store, and immediately, the regular checker looked in their direction; they kept walking toward the back of the store and headed for the deli section. The cashier turned on the microphone, which made a loud beeping noise that could be heard throughout the store, "Code 3 to check stand 5...Code 3 to check stand 5". That was the code, which meant it was the end of one cashier's shift, and they needed the replacement to come and fill in.

    Iesha was in the back talking to Jeff, the store's head manager. Jeff was relatively short for a man and held such a serious stature most of the time. He was a pretty fair boss, but some of his ways and attitude made Iesha wonder if Jeff liked other men. There were times when she had witnessed Jeff feeling upset over something or another, and he would place his hands on his hips in a way that looked feminine to her. She had also witnessed him snap his fingers while making a statement and was convinced after that. She had just finished telling him of her friend who had just been released from prison but was working very hard to get his life together and wanted to know if there were any open positions there at the Food Mart.

Jeff rested his chin on his palm while listening to Iesha's story. Jeff already had his answer set in his mind before she had even finished asking. Jeff paused before beginning, then looked at Iesha from behind his thick glasses and asked in a serious tone, "Say, if I were to hire this friend of yours, would you assume the liability for him and any mistakes that he may make?" Iesha knew what Jeff was imposing by asking her this question, but she still asked anyway, "What mistakes are you referring to, Jeff?" Jeff rolled his eyes and smirked a little as he cocked his head to one side, "Oh, you know what I mean, Iesha. Are you forgetting the past incidents that occurred when we tried to be fair and hire people regardless of a criminal background history, like the many incidents of sticky fingers? The cash register is coming up short on a more than average basis, Oh! Oh, and let's not forget my favorite, them coincidentally forgetting to lock up after closing, and we get robbed in the middle of the night?" Jeff dramatically placed his hands on both sides of his face as he spat out the last statement. He looked at Iesha and shook his head slowly for a second before continuing, "All I am saying is that if we were to hire your friend and something like that happened to us again, your job may be on the line because of it." Iesha looked at Jeff, and while her temper was seething underneath, she stayed cool on the surface, showing no extra emotions. She knew all too well that Jeff had a point, and the truth was that she could not afford to risk herself and her career on Joose. "Okay, Jeff, I guess I will let him know that we don't have any openings right now." She half smiled, then walked away. Jeff chimed in after her, "We do have openings...but are you confident in your friends' integrity, Iesha? Now, that is the real question." Jeff stated as he snapped his fingers and formed an invisible question mark in the air before him. Iesha looked back at Jeff and responded dryly, "I'm not sure; I will have to get back to you on that after I have thought it over more carefully." "Sure, Iesha, but if you say yes, he's in as far as I'm concerned; let me know by the end of the week."

"Okay, sure thing."

Iesha left the small office near the restrooms in response to the page that rang out almost five minutes ago. She knew that Rene' was waiting for her to relieve her from her shift as usual; as she headed toward the front of the store, she noticed two homeless-looking individuals slowly walking down the bread aisle. What drew her attention to them was that she heard loud, raspy whispering coming from the man saying something like "Hurry up!" She decided to approach them. As she came about five feet within their space, her nose was acutely aware of the stench that was coming from the both of them; it was enough to make her gag and stop in her tracks. She placed a hand in front of her mouth to keep the Frankie's Double Cheeseburger she had for lunch from coming up out of her stomach. Without saying a word, she turned to head toward the front register. "Hurry up and grab us some soda, dummy! You won't do nothin' if I don't tell you to, will ya?" C-Low spat out at Jackie in his usual harsh tone; she hurriedly ran over to the next aisle and stuffed four sodas into the inside arm spaces of her jacket.

There were so many holes inside the lining that she had begun using the spaces to her advantage; she realized that she could stuff things into her jacket, and they would become lost inside the tangle of pockets and rips, so to the point that she would have to take off her jacket and shake it out to get the things that she had put inside of it. C-Low walked past the candy section on his way toward the exit, grabbed about five candy bars in one hand, and shoved them down into his shirt, which was tucked inside his pants as if it were an oversized pocket. He already had a loaf of bread stuffed inside of his shirt, a pack of cheese, and two packs of hot dogs. He was aware of the fact that he appeared just to be a dirty bum with a lot of extra clothing on, and in cases like this one, he was thankful for the misconception that most people held toward him and that no one really knew that most of the time the extra clothing was what he used to cover the fact that he usually had stolen goods or something else that he was not supposed to have somewhere on him. C-Low stood beside the magazine section, right near the grocery carts and the exit, waiting for Jackie to come near him so they could walk out together. Ever since they had been down with each other, they committed that they never left each other, no matter what; Jackie had C-Low's back regardless of the situation, and he had her back the same way. Jackie came up next to C-Low and nodded her head, which was silent communication between them, indicating that all was well and they could leave the store. Both of them headed for the door, and just as they neared the exit, one of the packs of hot dogs fell out of the bottom of C-Low's raggedy shorts and hit the floor, making a small slapping sound and causing the cashier and assistant manager to look up from counting the money at the register. Iesha immediately realized what was happening and, knowing that she was obligated to protect the store's merchandise, loudly yelled, "Hey, what do you have in your jacket?" As she began to run from behind the counter, she was prepared to wrestle the man all by herself if she had to. C-Low suddenly broke into a run toward the door; Jackie only stood frozen in place beside the magazines, unsure of what to do. Just as C-Low reached the exit and pushed his way through to his escape, Iesha was about five feet behind the doors and screaming loudly, "Empty your damn pockets, you thief! Bring your ass back here!" As Iesha emerged through the doors, she was unprepared for what would happen next.

Joose, apparently on his way to the Food Mart to talk to the owner that afternoon, walked right into the situation. The filthy bum ran right into Joose and hit the ground in his clumsiness. Iesha was still yelling and was so worked up that she did not even recognize her cousin at the moment. Joose's time in prison had given him the skills to quickly and instantly evaluate crazy situations, and he knew exactly what was going on.

He quickly grabbed C-Low by his coat jacket collar as he struggled to get up off of the ground. "Alright, alright, old man, just empty your pockets…ain't nobody got to go to jail today or nothin' like that; just give the manager back the stuff you done stole, and everything will be cool, right?" Joose was on all fours, holding C-Low down as he struggled to get up from underneath Joose's muscular weight. By this time, a small crowd was beginning to form, and Jackie had slowly snuck outside the store and was standing off to one side. She did not want to leave C-Low, but she knew she had better get away from the scene if they had any food to eat later. She slowly began to edge away from the crowd unnoticed, and when she got far enough down the block, she turned the corner and broke into a run. She felt the weight of all the food items and canned sodas in her jacket, and she was slowed down by it. She felt as if she wished she were dead with how life was for her right now.

Her feet were searing with pain and it felt as though someone were using scratch paper to rip the soles from her feet due to the many holes in her shoes and the scorching hot ground making it nearly unbearable to take another step. She did her best to mentally phase out of her mind how excruciating the pain was that she felt right now both physically and spiritually. Jackie mentally pushed the pain to the back of her mind as usual, and she allowed herself to feel a small twang of relief at the sight of the bridge that she and C-Low called home coming closer and closer into view. "Won't be long now, Jackie, just a few more steps and we'll be home". She spoke aloud to herself, encouraging her body to make it the rest of the way. The heat was sweltering to the point that Jackie felt as if she would melt, being bundled up inside of the large, dirty and stinky, trench coat that she was wearing which had now become a part of her everyday apparel. She was now only ten feet away from the makeshift shelter that the two had created under the bridge which was where they laid their heads each night. They had found this section of the bridge which was unoccupied and very near the end of the freeway structure all the way to the back. The day that they decided this would be their new home, she and C-Low went over to the local laundry mat and stole some blankets and sheets out of a dryer that someone had left unattended in which to set up their new dwelling place. There just so happened to be poles all over the place in various areas underneath the bridge and this made a perfect way for them to fashion some make shift walls. It was Jackie's idea to tie the blankets to the poles with some kite string; she fastened the ends of the blankets one by one to the poles at the top, center and bottom. She had worked hard to fasten the blankets as securely as possible at the bottom so that wind or cold air would not seep through. The couple had also gone out the same day and looked fervently for other items that could be added to their new home, they found carpet which had been discarded from a vacant apartment nearby, and a couple of small broken dressers with only one drawer missing. One of the dresser's served as the storage for their food, and the other was used to store various items and everything from crack pipes and lighters to knives, rocks or any other defense mechanisms that the two found handy to use against others if and when it became necessary.

When Jackie finally reached the tent (as she sometimes called it), she nearly collapsed from heat exhaustion and pain. As she fell to her knees near one corner of the tent, she hurriedly worked to remove the oversized trench coat, and once it was off, she threw it to the side. Next, her attention was drawn to her feet, which were by now so enveloped with pain that they nearly felt numb. She slowly removed her tattered tennis shoes one after the other and twisted up her feet so that she could inspect the damage; both feet had circular-shaped holes burned into the bottoms in three to four different areas, which matched the holes in the bottoms of her shoes. The skin was completely torn off of the soles on her feet, exposing bright red bleeding, sore and tender meat which was dotted with tiny rocks, dirt, and other debris, only adding to the pain and irritation that she now felt.

In her anger and frustration, she slowly began to shake her head back and forth in disbelief about the life she was now living. She could not believe that this was really her life. She thought back to the many times that she had passed up homeless people on the streets, either begging for money or nonchalantly strolling along the walkway, and how she would think to herself that they were so pitiful and weak-minded to allow themselves to succumb to such a trifling way of living, and now look; she was one of them. Jackie began to let the tears fall from her face; rocking back and forth, she thought about how she was only afforded this luxury when she was alone because C-Low would get angry at her for any display of what he called "weak emotions." Weak emotions consist of things such as crying, complaining, or even speaking in an ill manner regarding their present circumstances. C-Low always told her, "The situation is what it is, period, point blank! There's no sense cryin' bout it; might as well work through it." Most of the time, he just so happened to be snatching her up by the back of her hair, and he yelled this on her face. Jackie yelled out in her fury; just the thought of C-Low and how abusive he was to her made her sick to her stomach. She had asked herself many, many times about the reason why she had been willing to live like this for so long? It seemed as if she were becoming the very things she had despised her whole life.

She had a brief flashback about her crack-headed grandmother and drunken grandfather, him slapping her in the face as a child, and her grandmother forced her to prostitute at only twelve years old. Jackie was already messed up in the mind and heart when she turned 18 and found out that she was adopted. Jackie always found herself daydreaming about who her natural parents may have been and, even more so, why her parents or mother gave her up for adoption. The loneliness that always seemed to surround her was the reason why she had always been desperate for attention and affection. Usually willing to do anything for attention, Jackie had always found herself in bad situations where she was being used or abused and taken advantage of. She had always played the follower role and not the leader in life, always easily swayed by others' opinions of who she was and not the one to live life fearlessly or without risk of rejection. She was just beginning to discover who she was on the inside and just beginning to feel like she was valuable when she met C-Low. Every since he had come into her life, things had been forever made different.

She had gone from being a high-powered office manager for the State of Colorado's Transportation Department to an abused, homeless, and scandalous drug addict seemingly overnight. As she sat on the floor and wailed aloud, Jackie, for the moment, was unable to do anything else but rock back and forth in one spot as she gently rubbed her throbbing and pain-seared feet. Jackie quickly silenced herself as she heard a sound from outside the tent. She sat stiffly and strained her ears to listen, almost sure that her sensitively trained ears had picked up the sound of some nearby movement; just when she was about to loosen up and disregard the sound, there it was again like someone's feet were shuffling within ten feet of her. Jackie sat holding her breath as the footsteps grew closer and closer; now, whoever was approaching was right outside of her tent. She felt a knot growing in her stomach as she wondered who could be approaching her home. She knew it was not C-Low because he had a horrible habit of snorting every few seconds, and if it were him, he would have snorted by now. Jackie slowly began to edge over to the weapons cabinet, and just as she began to slide little by little, someone quickly snatched open the blanket and began shining a bright light into her eyes so that she could not make out who it was.

"Freeze and put your hands in the air!" A strong male voice yelled at Jackie, a police officer in full uniform, who was now inside her tent. Jackie put both hands in the air, instinctively blocking her face and eyes from the bright light, not sure what to think; all of her years of thievery had finally caught up with her, she reasoned. "The damn police officer must have followed me from the store," she thought to herself. The police officer quickly made his way over to Jackie and began to pat her down with one hand; as he held the gun on her with the other, Jackie briefly noted his name tag, which read Officer Darius Tyson. "What did I do? I didn't do anything offissssa' Please…What's goin' on?" Jackie began to wail in a high pitched and sad voice. "Who else is in here? I heard someone screaming!" The officer demanded his questions in a forceful and unsympathetic tone, seemingly unmoved by Jackie's pleas'. By this time he had at least lowered the flashlight so that Jackie could make out his features. Tall, with light brown skin and light brown eyes, she noticed that he was very attractive but also very arrogant. "Offissa, I'm the only one here that was me you heard screamin'. I was just cryin', is all." Officer Tyson's face softened a little, and Jackie could sense in his demeanor that his guard had also dropped a little concerning her. "Why were you crying? What is your name?" The officer still had some gruffness in his tone and sounded as if he were exaggerating the professionalism still displayed in his hostile stature. "Why do you care? Nobody cares bout' me no more!" Jackie screamed out at the officer; her sudden outburst caught the young officer off guard, and he instinctively reached for his pistol. He realized she did not mean him any harm, but he did not want to take any chances. "What's goin on? Tell me your story. You got two minutes to start talking; now speak up!" The officer's voice was a little softer but still very demanding. Jackie realized that he was going to be a cop, maybe a nice cop, but a cop nevertheless.

Jackie sat in silence for a moment; this could be her chance, her chance to get some help for herself and her situation, a chance to really leave C-Low like she had always dreamed of, a chance to get off of the drugs, get clean again and really get herself together. Or it could be her worst nightmare; she could go to prison for the drugs, or C-Low would find out she had been talking to this cop and try to kill her. Jackie sat still in a state of confusion, unsure what to do. It was a well known fact in this day and age that conversation of any kind with the police was highly prohibited in the streets. If anyone saw you conversating with a black and white, you were lucky if you did not end up dead later on the same week. Hell or high water-nobody played the game with neighborhood snitches.

Chapter 9

C-Low had been on the ground for nearly five whole minutes; a group of about fifteen to twenty people gathered around the scene, mostly teenagers and other young people, laughing hilariously at him lying on the ground and struggling to get up.

He was boiling on the inside with pure rage; how dare this fool do him like this? Didn't he know who he was dealing with? "Git up offa' me! C-Low yelled, "You don't know who I am? I will have you taken out nigga... damn you! Damn you!" The scrawny bum struggled and tried with all his strength to maneuver out from up under Joose's grip. As the skinny man continued straining and thrusting, trying to outmaneuver Jooses grip, he was mumbling unintelligible slurs and partial sentences that made no sense..." Nigga you almost was me, and I coulda been you.... oooohhhh.... let me get up, let me get atcha... ooohhh imma get you! Imma gettt youuuu!"

Joose found it amusing that the tall, wispy, homeless looking drug addict thought that he was so tough. He guessed it was all a part of his crackhead fantasy reality; Joose couldn't help but laugh on the inside at the efforts of the small yet tall man who was trying with all of his might to get himself up off of the ground but could not. Finally, Joose began to climb up off the ground while still holding the collar of the skinny man, trying his best to keep a straight face and not burst out laughing; he calmly began addressing the bum, "Hey man, just relax a little bit, and everything will be alright, we gon' straighten this out aight?" Joose looked into the man's face. Although he had initially thought for some reason the man was older, he realized that his face was that of a younger man, weatherbeaten from the drugs, and looking into his eyes foretold a sad story of growing up young and hard in the lonely streets of poverty and the ghetto. The man stared back at Joose in such a way that it caused the strange feeling of deja' vue to swell up in his gut, did this man know him from somewhere? Was he ever in one of the joints with him or something? Joose didn't recognize him and couldn't tell if he knew him from passing or not, and quite possibly, he did not know the unfortunate soul at all.

Joose released the man's collar and helped him get up off of the ground; the homeless man snatched his arm away from Joose and looked back at him with a look of sheer hatred in his eyes. "Wasup, man? Why are you out here stealing like this anyway? Why don't you just go on ahead and empty those pockets, and then you can be on ya way, now that's option number one, or you can take option number two, and I can hold ya black ass here until the Po-Po's arrive and they can cart your funky ass off to the county jail! Now, what's it gonna be? You got three minutes to take yo' pick!" Joose stood only inches away from C-Low; he had to fight with all of his muscle reflexes to keep from gagging on the stench of his body odor, which was so foul, putrid, and overwhelming that it was almost intoxicating. Joose could not imagine how it must be to live the way that this man had allowed himself to exist on a daily basis. C-Low looked down at the ground as his pride swelled from within him. He was aware that he held the trifling appearance of a filthy homeless bum, which was completely messed up from drugs and alcohol abuse. Inside C's mind, he is still the notorious gangster he used to be. Nobody could play C-Low; he was even surprised that this fool seemed so comfortable with disrespecting and making a joke out of him. C-Low thought quickly, no one usually expected him to be such a violent person, C-Low was aware of the fact that people grossly underestimated the intelligence and awareness that homeless people possessed. C-Low began to step back. He noticed the chump that was hemming him up and shot a quick glance toward the short, fat owner. C-Low guessed that he must have been trying to impress him or something. C-Low raised his right hand in the air before him, "Okay...I'm just gonna give you what I got so you'll let me go, Gotdamn, a nigga can't even get no bit of grub for dinner tonight, or nothin' huh?"

C-Low reached down into the left-hand side of his raggedy coat liner, suddenly pulled out a shiny Chrome 45 Automatic, and quickly pointed it in Joose's face as he yelled, "Now was up, fool! You had everybody laughin' at me, and now the joke's on you, punk! Who's laughin' now? Huh? Huh?" He sang out as he formed a dark smile upon his chapped crusty lips, revealing teeth so yellow that they appeared to be coated in butter, as well as snaggle-toothed with several missing and the rest crooked; the result of drugs and neglect. He stood there, face and body dripping in sweat and reeking of the sweet/sour stench of human urine and feces...C-Low stepped forward and now had the tip of the gun to Joose's forehead, shoving it into his skin in a forceful manner as he gritted his teeth and growled in pleasure. He was enjoying the shift of this power dynamic tremendously.

Joose slowly brought both hands up over his head, and with his hands trembling, his life quickly flashed before his eyes as he closed them, anticipating the loud bang that was sure to follow. Everyone in the crowd began to gasp, shriek, and scream as they began backing away from the scene in fear of the bum turning the gun to the crowd and possibly firing random shots. A few people yelled, "Don't shoot... please don't!"

Iesha could hardly believe what was going on as she quickly thought about what, if anything, she could possibly do in this situation; she felt a little guilty that her cousin was putting himself in the line of danger all because he was trying to impress her into helping him. She made a quick decision, "Hey!" Iesha yelled in a high-pitched voice; everyone's attention was now zeroed in on her. "Why don't you just take the stuff and get the hell on away from here? If you don't leave now, I will call the police so we can have yo' ass arrested!" Iesha stood pointing her finger toward the opposite way almost even in the direction of C-Low's tent, emphasizing her final statement. C-Low was still standing holding the gun to Joose's face, as he began to laugh showing off even more of his crooked and rotting yellow-brown, stubby teeth, "Yeah, what go around come back around don't it bruh bruhhhh?" C-Low spat out in his garbled slang, drool dripping from his lips. Joose was barely able to understand him as he looked closer into the face of the man who would possibly kill him, "Now I'm on this end, but I used to be on that end… You memba'?" C-Low tossed the statement out of his mouth in a much louder voice than the previous statement as he stared Joose in the face, wondering how he dared to pretend like he didn't know him. C-Low jumped toward Joose and spat out in a loud voice, "Think hard, lil homie!.... Bang Bang Nigga! Hahahaahahah!" He laughed as he started running off in the direction of home.

He began running faster and faster, peering back and over his shoulder as he quickly made his way down the street; as soon as he rounded the corner, he tucked the shiny gun he had stolen months ago back inside his raggedy coat pocket. He had a quick flash of memory burst forth of the day that he'd stolen the gun from a game goofy businessman who had ignorantly parked his brand new Lincoln Towncar on one of the busy downtown streets; leaving his windows halfway rolled down, C-Low lurked in the nearby alleyway watching the man as he paid the meter up for a whole hour, and went inside the 'Sweet Love Motel,' no doubt cheating on his wife or girlfriend C-Low had supposed at the time. On that day, C-Low had hit a gold mine as he discovered the man's wallet in the glovebox, with credit cards included, as well as the gun and some cash, which was stashed underneath the seat inside of a neat, white envelope, freshly withdrawn from the bank.

The memory faded away quickly as it had come. As he continued sprinting down the street, he began to slow his pace as he approached and found himself within eye vision of the tent that he shared with Jackie. "Hotttt damn! Nows I gotta deal with that hoodrat dirty hoe ass Jackie!" C-Low spoke out loud to himself, still tingling with adrenaline as he realized that this was his first time even thinking about her since he looked over and watched her bail out on him when he had gotten busted earlier. C-Low felt himself getting excited and starting to form an erection at the thought of how good it would feel to release his frustrations by beating her up later on. He had a quick flashback of how her nose bled so very easily whenever he socked her in it and how very wimpy she was, as well as how she always just screamed, cried, and begged him to please have mercy on her and stop beating her. For some reason, her weak voice and pleas for mercy only made him want to beat her worse and worse; it gave him an adrenaline rush and pure joy as well because it was something that he absolutely loved to do. Usually, when he was done, and she was bloody with her face lumped up, swollen, and disfigured, he would force her to give him head, then have sex with her.

C-Low slowed his sprint to a light jog as his coat bounced up and down from being heavily weighed down by the stolen groceries he still held inside. He was now within thirty feet from the tent as he balled his fist up in anticipation of the beating that he was about to put down on Jackie, but he was not prepared for what took place next.

The crowd dissipated from the front of the Food Mart within minutes of C-Low running away. Iesha allowed her muscles to relax a little and felt her hurried heartbeat begin to slow to its normal pace as the immediate threat of the dangerous homeless thief was removed from the atmosphere. "I think I am going to call the police, just in case," Iesha stated to no one in particular as she headed back into the grocery store to use the phone in the rear of the store located in Jeff's office. Joose stood in the same spot as if glued in one place. He could not believe what had just happened, and his mind was still being bombarded with the statements that the bum had made before running off. The fact that a gun had been pulled on him was big enough all by itself because where Joose was from, everyone pretty much followed the same rules; you didn't pull a gun on someone unless you planned on shooting them. If you didn't shoot them, then you had better not be unfortunate enough to cross paths with that same person again, or else you might get killed yourself for attempting to bluff a threat. As far as Joose was concerned, the gun threat was not quite as unsettling as the remarks that the man had made to him.

He could not make out everything told to him, but he could comprehend that the bum knew him from somewhere. Usually, Joose stays on top of his game; he never forgets a face. Even if he briefly crosses paths with a person and never knows their name, he always remembers that person's face. This situation was somehow different. Joose felt a strange familiarity with the ways and demeanor of the bum, but he did not recognize his face at all. The only thought that seemed to make him the tiniest amount of sense was that this man must have been one of Joose's old celly's or some other unimportant person he had met during one of his many times in prison.

    Joose's eyes caught a glimpse of movement to his left, and his attention was drawn to Jeff, who was standing off near the side of the Food Mart; he had taken the liberty of pulling out a cigarette and lighting it, then placing his hands on his hips as he absent-mindedly watched Joose while he puffed on his cigarette. Joose looked back at him for a moment, unsure if he was the actual owner; his physique did not seem to carry much authority in it from what Joose could see. As if a light bulb had gone off in Jeff's head, he did a double take into Joose's face and snapped his finger before calling out, "Hey there, young man, can I ask you some questions about employment?" Joose turned and began to head toward Jeff at a slowed pace, outwardly showing that he was not completely comfortable at the moment. Jeff started by apologizing about what had happened, extending his hand and smiling. "Hi, Sir. My name is Jeffery Morgan. I am the store owner, and I want to deeply apologize that you had to fight off one of our thieves, but I would also like to say that I feel you handled the situation exceptionally well, and should you be available and interested, I would like to offer you a job here, as our stores new stocker and security guard." Joose felt himself growing excited inside but held himself back to figure out the complete details of what he would be signing up for. Joose didn't immediately respond, and Jeff looked at him in silence, awaiting his response to the job offer. Joose calmly replied, "Thank you, sir; I do appreciate the job offer; it couldn't have come at a better time, actually….. Could you please just give me more details about the position?" "Oh yes, definitely, here. Why don't we step into my office, and we can get better acquainted and go over all the terms, shall we?" Jeff gestured toward the store with a limp right wrist as Joose followed behind him into the store.

Chapter 10

"Yo, Willy! Willyyyy?" Dirty Black was yelling in a loud voice. He had just seen Willy across the hall a minute ago, more than likely creeping with Momma Greens. Momma Greens was also known as Big Momma G to all the gangsters of Garden Projects. Everyone viewed her as the hood's mother figure. She was well into her 60s but still down with the clique. She sold weed, babysat, sold plates of food, ran a candy house, and refereed fights and arguments. Out of all their years of knowing each other, Willy had never looked at G in that type of way but had here lately been spending more and more time at her home and in her company. Black closed the door with a loud bang and sat on the couch in a disturbed way. He had just gotten off the phone with Shawalli… he was the notorious Afghani drug lord whom the hood bought the majority of their products, and he was a cold-hearted gangsta. He had a trademark for eliminating the body parts of the people whom he had felt crossed him; there were rumors about Shawalli that ranged from him cutting out the tongues of people who had been caught lying to him and cutting off the hands of people who had stolen from him or cheated him in some way.

He had been doing business with Doctor Willy and Dirty Black for years, and they had never had any problems with one another because it was a well-known fact that both parties were equally feared and even held the same mutual respect for one another. In the drug business, trust was very hard-earned, and breaking a trust relationship at any time was grounds to be killed, but even more so, horribly tortured before your death to set a prime example for future reference. Shawalli was usually a mild-tempered person because he rarely acted hastily, gave himself time to premeditate his actions, and had no dealings with sloppy work or individuals. He had been under investigation for different allegations many times, but due to no witnesses willing to testify against him and no evidence found, law enforcement could never make any of the charges stick against him.

Dirty Black was shaken up due to the anger and hostility that had just been displayed in the phone call from Shawalli just minutes ago some new youngsta's that the clique had recently hired, had attempted to jack Shawalli for some credit on a product that he had made good on and delivered. As always, in these instances, Doctor Willy and Dirty Black were given a three-day grace period and would always deliver Shawalli's money which would yield no less than 20,000.00 per transaction; however, this transaction was going down a little different than usual, the youngsta's which included three teenagers; Ruthless who was the oldest at age 17, Lil Rick age 15, and the youngest in the crew was Alonzo at age 13, they were sent to meet up with Shawalli's thugs to pick up the Coke and deliver the money four days ago and had not been seen since.

According to Shawalli, his boys had made good on their end of the deal but were told by Doc's boys that the O.G said he needed three days to make good on his end, but in reality, Doctor Willy and Dirty Black had already given the money to the boys for them to complete the transaction. Since the drop was scheduled to take place on the West Coast in Stockton, CA. The G's knew that it would take one week of driving to arrive there and back from Jersey, so they were not immediately alarmed that a few days had passed with no word; that was to be expected if not a couple of extra days just for the rest during the long drive across the country.

In Dirty Black's mind, he could hardly believe this was going on and hoped deep down that there was some kind of mistake taking place and not these three young stupid baby g's gathering up enough courage to try and pull a major jack move on both Shawalli's clique and the Doctor's clique. This was something that had never been attempted by any member of the Mafia to date, no doubt, because everyone knew that it would be serious hell to pay for a double-cross like that. Also, you would be jeopardizing the welfare of your own family, all friends, and acquaintances because when the Mafia was after you, there was literally nowhere to run or hide that they did not have eyes watching.

"Son of a bitch!" Shawalli yelled as he pounded his fist on the small, shiny oak round table and slammed the phone onto the receiver, ending his conversation with Dirty Black. After many years of solid transactions between him and the Mafia, he had finally been burned, and now he had to come up with a plan of action; this was going to get very ugly, and very soon if his money did not materialize within the next 48 hours as he had just told Black. Shawalli stood at about six and a half feet, with a muscular build; he had jet black hair cut short and trimmed to perfection, blatantly revealing a scalp full of deep, dark waves. He was strikingly handsome and good-looking, but something in his eyes let you know you were in the presence of a dangerous man. Shawalli was so cruel that he was commonly called "Heartless" for a nickname.

He now sat listening to his opera music softly playing from the small speaker set on his desk, which almost completely masked the vague sounds of high pitch screaming coming from the basement as the boys who had been sent to do the drop were now being punished for allowing the goods to be given with no money crossing palms instead of calling him right away to tell him about the situation. The young men were actually over the age of twenty years old but were still regarded as boys to Shawalli because they had no idea of just how badly they had jeopardized their own lives by taking on employment with him and his foul company of lowdown killers. The crew leader responsible for doing the drop was now screaming at the top of his lungs as one of Shawalli's henchmen; Pablo was excitedly using a rusty pair of pliers to rip his fingernails out one at a time. Socrates' was in excruciating agony and pain as his fingernails were being torn from his skin one by one, blood was dripping and spewing out of his fingertips in every direction, and at this moment, he could do nothing more than reflect back on the careless decision that he had made. His inner gut was warning him not to give over the product without receiving the money as planned, but Ruthless from Doc's crew was someone that he had dealt with on a few previous occasions, and as far as anyone knew, his word was pretty solid. Socrates did not want to seem like an amateur by stopping everything to call Shawalli, so he completed the transaction all on his own, hoping that he was showing he could deal with unexpected situations like these and, therefore, step his rank up. Little did he know that no one could be trusted in the streets, especially when it came to doing business with so much Coke and money involved.

    Honor and loyalty should never be expected, so he was now learning his first harsh lesson about trust. His four fingers on his left hand were swelling to twice their original sizes, and now Pablo was locking the pliers onto Socrates' left thumb; he slowly began to pull and twist the nail which was locked within the pliers, as the flesh started to rip and the fingernail began to separate from Socrates' finger, Pablo licked his lips in anticipation of the loud moan that he knew was soon to follow. The bloody finger, which was now searing with pain and showing bright red meat from beneath the former fingernail, released a small mist of blood that squirted Pablo in the face, barely missing his right eye; at this, he smiled widely as he drank in the details of Socrates' horrified face and his mouth as it slowly twisted into a fresh new pain filled scream, full of sheer terror and untold human suffering. Socrates would never forget this horrible lesson issued to him at the hands of his boss, Shawalli.

Chapter 11

Jackie quickly weighed up her options, reasoning within herself that she had silently prayed for some kind- or any kind of resolution to her messed up life so many times, and now it could be right here before her very eyes if she chose to come clean. Only God himself knew how badly she wanted things to change, but C-Low was the only thing that stood in her way. She hesitated a few seconds longer out of the fear of the punishment that he would bestow on her; even if she did manage to escape him and this horrible life that had wrapped its way around her, she knew that she could never escape C-Low, he was the type that kept a grudge and if you burnt him, he would definitely come to find you. "Well... I'm waiting!" The officer stated in such a loud tone that it caused Jackie to jump a little. He impatiently watched her as she gathered her thoughts, "Well, you see, offissa...I used to be a real important person, I worked for the State of Colorado and everythang, but I got wrapped up with the wrong person and now..." Jackie allowed her voice to trail off as she held her arms out before her in a gesture that non verbally told him, 'Now look at me.' The officer stood there for a few moments without speaking; he put one hand to his chin and asked Jackie in a serious tone, "Why haven't you gotten any help for yourself? Are you happy living like this? Surely you must want better?" Jackie let a few seconds pass as she mentally tried to summon the words that would begin to tell the officer about C-Low, her at-one-time lover, current abuser, and, to a certain extent, her captor. No one knew C-Low like Jackie did; she knew a lot about him just from spending years with him and what he had opened up and told her about his past before he met her. She knew he had been in the streets his entire life and had gotten messed up in the process. He had suffered mental breakdowns and lost family and close friends due to some of his street dealings and involvements. He had even gotten hooked on crack, methamphetamine, and other hardcore drugs. C-Low had, in fact, become a homeless bum who had smoked out on Coke for many years before he had met her.

Just as Jackie opened her mouth to speak to the cop, the curtain to the tent was suddenly snatched back, with C-Low emerging through the entrance, yelling out in a loud voice and pointing his filthy finger at her... "Bitch Yo' assssss is mines now!" The words had escaped his mouth before he noticed the police officer standing in the corner of the tent; if he had paid special attention, he would have noticed the police car parked right in front of the freeway exit near the bridge's entrance. C-Low froze in place with his finger suspended in mid-air; his eyeballs were widened almost double the size of their usual protrusion as he looked the officer in the face, unable to process and understand exactly what was happening. His first thought was that the bitch must have set him up. Officer Tyson quickly grabbed his gun from the holster, "Put your hands in the air!" He yelled out as he sharply pointed his revolver toward C-Low's face. C-Low raised both hands in the air as he shot a surprised and angry look at Jackie. Jackie now had tears in her eyes as she held her mouth wide open in shock and only shook her head back and forth, not knowing anything else to do and not wanting to look back at C-Low. Technically, she had not done anything against him yet; he had done it himself by coming home ready to beat her for what happened earlier. The officer quickly shoved his gun back into his holster as he grabbed both of C-Low's arms and secured them behind his back, practicing a maneuver he had done many times to perfection as he quickly slid on a pair of shiny handcuffs onto C-Low's wrists, he then began to pat him down seemingly unaware of the overwhelmingly foul odor that was attached to his body. The officer felt many items in C-Low's coat and went through his gnarled and mangled pockets one at a time. Officer Tyson began to pull out the food items first, one after the other, candy bars, hot dog wieners, bread; shaking his head, he spoke to C-Low..." Judging from all this food, looks like you just robbed the grocery store down the street, you'll be getting arrested for misdemeanor petty theft for sure..." he stated as he continued feeling around C-Low's raggedly torn garments. He then reached over and felt the hard steel of a gun protruding from C-Low's left pocket. Removing the gun, the officer sang sarcastically, "Well, well, well...... what do we have here?" He emphasized his last statement. Jackie only stood across the room, watching with wide eyes, unable to believe what was taking place. She was trying to wrap her mind around the concept that C-Low would be getting arrested and more than likely going to prison, and at the very least, he would be surely going to county jail, but going away, he would be nonetheless. Officer Tyson pulled the small intercom from the attached strap near his shoulder and pressed the button, sending a loud, thin, chirping noise into the atmosphere. "Dispatch to Officer Tyson, go ahead." "Yes, I am located underneath the 63rd Street freeway exit beneath the overpass back near the rear; I have a male suspect in possession of an illegal firearm, as well as possession of stolen items; please send backup A.S.A.P."

Officer Tyson grabbed his gun and held it steady as he kept his eyes upon C-Low's face, with his gaze locked on to C-Low's. "Copy that backup is on the way." The female dispatcher's voice snapped back in response. Officer Tyson began to read C-Low his Miranda Rights... "You have the right to remain silent; anything you say can and will be used against you; you have the right to an attorney."

Officer Tyson's voice faded into the background in Jackie's mind, and as she was no longer looking at C-Low, she was now sitting on the floor and silently rocking back and forth in one spot as her thoughts drifted away. A million questions flooded her mind seemingly at once, 'How is this possible? Is this real... she wasn't passed out dreaming, was she?' She lightly pinched herself just to be sure; it definitely wouldn't be the first time her mind had played this cruel trick on her. 'Ouch,' she thought to herself. She was awake, and this was happening. 'What would life be like without C-Low? Would she be able to get herself together and clean of her cocaine habit after being down like this for so long? Would he possibly just leave her alone and go on without her? It was all too much to even hope for, she thought vaguely.

Just then C-Low's voice rang out, "Bitch...I shoulda' known not ta' trust yo' dirty ass. You set me up! You just wait tho' you gon' get yowes....you gonna get it dirty bitch!" C-Low dragged out the last statement while grinding his teeth and looking at Jackie, "Hey, you shut the hell up!" Officer Tyson cut in, "Where I'm taking your ass to you wont be able to 'get' nobody. You better hope nobody don't 'get' your ass!" The officer held a small twist of humor in his tone, but his authority made it perfectly clear he was not to be crossed.

C-Low stood there with his face twisted into a bitter scowl; his mind raced with dozens of possible outcomes for his present situation as he fantasized about the possibility of getting away. In one scenario, he saw himself trying to twist around and grab the officer's gun; in another, he saw himself lunging toward Jackie and violently biting her ankles until blood gushed everywhere; and in still another, he saw himself breaking into a ferocious run despite the fact that he was now handcuffed. As the officer finished reading him his rights, it began to hit home for C-Low that he was really being arrested. His mind began to search even faster for some answers to this new problem that he was facing; he could not realistically see himself doing another drop of time in the county jail, or even worse, Prison...but as things were looking, that was definitely what was taking place.

Jackie, silently staring at the floor, slowly lifted her eyes to look over at C-Low, wondering what he must be thinking at this moment. She knew him all too well, and if she knew him like she figured she did, he was busy planning an alternate route for going to jail. Jackie watched C-Low's eyes dart back and forth inside of his eye sockets as he looked from the officer to his gun to the floor. The rotation was fast and quick; that was how C-Low looked when he was brainstorming over something; there was no telling what would happen next; as Jackie continued to watch C-Low, feeling one hundred percent certain that something was about to take place, she lowered her eyes to the floor as the same old familiar nervous, nauseous feeling began to overwhelm her and make her feel sickly. Nervous butterflies performed a silent masquerade from within her. She could be wrong, but when she felt this way inside, she was usually left only wishing she had been wrong.

Chapter 12

Iesha now had a splitting headache; she took the liberty of sitting down for a few minutes at Jeff's desk to calm her nerves before she made the call to the police station. She silently told herself she might go home early today; the drama was too much on her nerves. She did not really want even to call the police, but she knew that in situations like these, it was store policy to at least report the incident so that it would be on file for future reference and insurance issues, as well as safety precautionary measures. Iesha reached toward the small black office phone on Jeff's desk but found her hand resists in mid-air. Always the one to assess her feelings, Iesha allowed her hand to draw back as she sat a few more minutes to analyze her feelings. She realized that she was not just shaken up at the robbery that had just unfolded; she was also very upset at the way everything went down. She did not feel comfortable that Joose was at the wrong place at the wrong time; she just had to step into the situation the way he did. Iesha was unsure of whether or not the feelings she was now experiencing were selfish or justified. She could not fight the anger threatening to rise within her at the thought of Joose jumping in the way he did, knowing that he only did it to sway Iesha's decision to hook him up. She knew that she was now in a situation where Joose may have felt she owed him a favor and did not like it.

Iesha began to tremble a little from the anger that was now rising up within her as she made up her mind that she was going to literally tell Joose off in a royal way if he asked her again about the hookup; she could almost hear him going home only to call her within hours to ask her what she thought of him playing the captain to save her. She wanted him to know for future reference that she was used to handling her own around the Food Mart and that if he had not shown up when he did, she would have chased that bum for a whole mile or more if she had to in order to recover the store's merchandise.

Iesha shook her head from side to side as she thought about it to herself; she would not be surprised if that man just so happened to be somebody that Joose hired to pull the robbery so that he could walk into it and make himself look good. How else could it have been timed so perfectly? The more and more she thought about it, it made perfect sense; everything added up now, all of it, from the pitiful bum struggling to get up off of the ground to him pulling the gun on Joose so that everything was all the more dramatic in its happening, yes it must have been a fake set up situation she assured herself. Iesha felt her adrenaline begin to subside as she found herself looking at today's robbery in a whole new light. She knew that Joose could be trifling, but staging a robbery to get the hookup, she did not realize that he would be willing to stoop so low to force her hand. She thought about it some more with a slight grin beginning to play over her face; if she allowed her assumptions to leak into Jeff's ears, then she would never have to worry about her cousin working alongside her or even getting close enough to rub elbows with her for that matter.

She decided to phone the police department in line with protocol despite her growing assumptions; the phone had rang for the eighth time before someone answered, "Newark P.D., How can I help you today?" The woman on the other line sounded bored with her position. "Yes, I need to report a robbery which took place at my site of employment today." Iesha held the line as she mentally prepared for the list of questions that would follow any second. Just as the woman on the other line was requesting the address, Jeff barged into his office with a wide smile on his face, "Hang up the phone Iesha, we won't be needing to file our usual complaint, things will be going differently from now on." Iesha felt the small pinch of irritation that was beginning to swell from within the back of her mind, as she lowered the phone from her mouth, "Jeff, what are you talking about? You know that we have to report this burglary as a part of standard procedure, don't you?" Iesha watched Jeff in anticipation of his answer, he only stood there with the smile on his face now transforming into a light grin as he placed one hand on his hip and brought the other to his face, sticking his pinky finger into the side of his mouth he began slightly pulling on his bottom lip in a teasing way, this action only added to Iesha's frustration as she watched him and actively thought about how feminine he appeared to be at this very moment. "Iesha…" Jeff exaggeratedly rolled his eyes toward the ceiling while shaking his head in feigned frustration, as he dropped the hand at his mouth to his other hip, "I don't know if I can call what happened today a robbery, or if I should refer to it as a blessing in disguise." Jeff allowed his voice to trail off as he began to slowly pace across the room heading toward his desk where Iesha still sat holding the phone. "As of today, we just may have a new crewmember on our team." Jeff raised his arms and gestured toward the door, at that moment Joose walked in to the small office area and stood next to Jeff, the two men seemed to be eagerly watching Iesha's face in anticipation of her reaction. Iesha slowly lowered the phone from her ear and sat it in the cradle as she returned Jeff's gaze unsure of which response she would choose to reply with. She felt her temper rising at the thought of Joose coming to work at the same place as she would be working every day, and although she was not entirely sure why she was feeling this way, she knew that she did not like the thought of him working up close with her.

Iesha tried to steady her voice and stifle the emotions threatening to burst forth at any given moment, "Congratulations!" She choked out from behind a phony smile. "Are you going to follow the standard hiring process and do an interview? Or are you just going to bring him on board right away?" She asked, looking at Jeff. Iesha waited for Jeff's response, and at the same time, she allowed another part of her mind to begin devising a way that she could possibly sabotage the plan for her cousin to gain employment alongside her. She desperately wanted her cousin to succeed and see him working, being independent, and taking care of himself, but not at her expense. "Hmmmmm... I am very tempted to say screw the standard hiring process, and let's just get this guy on deck right away! How does that sound to you?" Iesha did not know how to respond, so she just sat in silence, even thinking that in a worst-case scenario, if Joose did get hired by Jeff, the decision would be Jeff's own doing. He could in no way hold her reliable for any mistakes or mishaps that may occur while Joose was employed by the Food Mart. Joose stood in silence while watching Iesha's demeanor; he purposefully allowed his gaze to penetrate her because he knew she was fully aware that her word could make or break the chance that Jeff was giving him right now. He knew that she did not really want him working there, and he also knew better than to disclose the fact that they were related. He watched his cousin's hesitance, and he wondered why she felt this way toward helping him out. Still, he said nothing and just looked on.

The sheer thought of Joose being around her every day disgusted Iesha nonetheless, and she felt herself feeling bitter, angry, and resentful toward her cousin. Why did he have to come to her for help anyway? Couldn't he have gone some place else looking for a job? The questions bombarded Iesha's mind one after the other; she momentarily pushed them to the side as she resolved within herself that she would have to go home and sleep on all of today's events. Iesha knew that she was doing a lousy job of masking her feelings, as she just stood there with a silent, blank look on her face, allowing her eyes to dart back and forth from Jeff to Joose slowly. Jeff's still questioning eyes continued to linger on Iesha's face; as assistant manager, he sincerely wanted her honest standpoint regarding his offering of the job to Joose; when she did not respond, he loudly snapped his fingers, "Hello! I said 'What do you think?'". Jeff snapped in an irritable tone. Shaking her head, Iesha replied, "Ohh, I'm sorry Jeff, there's just so much goin on right now, uh… yeah that sounds good! It will be good to have you on board with us". Iesha smiled and nodded in Joose's direction, being fake as ever and feeling lousy because of it. She was now actually beginning to feel slightly sick to the stomach; she looked at her watch and noted that it was only a quarter to five p.m. Iesha then excused herself and left Jeff to talk with Joose; she headed toward the restroom, trying to escape the madness that still seemed to be going on.

The good thing about it all was that it was Friday, and she would have the whole weekend to herself; her appointment at Lynn's Nails was scheduled for the next morning, and with the long week that she had endured, her bi-weekly pampering session was very much needed. As she sat in the stall for a few moments, Iesha decided to do something that was out of the ordinary for her; she decided to leave work early and just take the rest of the evening off. She would have to wake up early for class tomorrow, but other than that she would be free for the entire evening. She began to feel happiness stirring within her at some new plans that were coming into view inside of her mind's eye; it occurred to her at that moment that she worked way too hard most of the time; she did not remember the last time that she had done anything leisurely to enjoy herself. Her thoughts skipped over to Jamar Washington, he was a fine, young, tall, and brown-skinned brother that had been really trying hard to get close to her here lately.

She'd met him about three months ago when he had come into the Coffee House one morning to get a Latte' evidently on his way to work. It seemed to her that they had made an instant connection, and the chemistry between them was so thick it could be cut with a knife. They had exchanged phone numbers back then and had been talking every since. Due to Iesha being the type of woman who was so self-spoiled and self indulgent, she usually had a hard time finding a man who enjoyed conversating about the same types of things that she did, such as the latest fashion designs, celebrity gossip, and plans of a rich future that sounded so flamboyant they were usually mistaken for wishful thinking when in the ears of other hearers, but Jamar was truly one of a kind. He appeared to be almost like a male version of herself, a type of man she had never encountered before. Just then, as if on cue, her phone rang, and it was Jamar calling, a wide smile spread across Iesha's face as she held a brief mental image of her plans for the evening falling into place. Iesha answered her phone in the usual manner, "Wasup wit it?" Jamar responded with his usual light humor, "Girl, it's all about you right now, you tell me wasup!" He laughed a little following his response, "What you getting' into tonight?" Iesha paused momentarily, not wanting to sound too eager to see him, "Uhh well, my home girl Keisha asked me to go out to the club down on Lakewood, but I told her I would have to think about it... Why? What you getting into later on?" Jamar did not try to hide the exaggerated disappointment in his voice; he had planned on hooking up with Iesha and hopefully finding himself spending the night with her. He had been playing it cool for three months now, but he knew she was feeling him the same way, and usually it never took him this long to get down with a woman, but as he was discovering, Iesha was no ordinary woman; she was special. "Oh, okay, so you tryin to go out shakin' that big old booty tonight, huh?" Jamar slid the statement out in a joking way, but there was plenty of jealousy playing on the undertones of his statement; Iesha caught it all but, for some reason, was humored by it, although she should have been concerned. It was way too early in the game for Jamar to be bothered by her whereabouts, and normally, Iesha would have been real quick to let a brother know not to come at her that way, but in Jamar's case, she felt like his reaction was further security about the way he felt for her. "I said I might! Do you know what might means? It means I may or may not go." Iesha responded in nonchalant sarcasm; she then added, "Why are you so concerned? It's not as if you have presented me with any alternative plans?" Jamar smiled and responded, "Well, that is why I decided to hit you up. I wanted to see if you felt like kickin' it with a brotha tonight…?" Iesha, again not wanting to sound happy or excited even though she was bubbling with anticipation and happiness at the thought of seeing him tonight responded dryly, "Kickin' it and doin what, may I ask?" "I was thinking that you may enjoy coming to my house and feasting on one of my home-cooked meals, watching a movie, and maybe having a few drinks with me." Jamar purposely added a seductive sounding tone to his voice as he emphasized his last statement, making sure that Iesha caught the drift of his true plans for the evening.

Iesha had never been to Jamar's house, but she knew that he lived by himself and considered himself a bachelor. He often talked about how he had to go home and clean his house or re-organize his living room and things of that nature. Iesha knew within herself that if she agreed to go, they would no doubt end up having sex tonight. "Hmm, it sounds like it may be fun; I'm gon have to think it over and get back to you, okay?" She already knew within herself that she was more than likely going to go, but she always enjoyed the ball being in her court, so she was not about to agree so easily. "Alright, beautiful, you think it over but don't keep me on hold too long, holla back so I don't go home and start hookin up that Flame Broiled T-bone Steak, Red Roasted Potatoes, Stir-fried veggies, and Cherry Pie with whipped cream for desert…all for nothing, aight?... You need to let a king spoil you tonight!" Jamar crooned smoothly, then hung up without another word. Iesha removed the phone from her ear and looked at the receiver, knowing she heard him hang up but not sure; she smiled as she placed the phone back into her front pants pocket. She quickly thought about what she could wear to see him tonight, knowing it would have to be something extra sexy that showed her cleavage and thighs; maybe she would go to the mall and pick out something brand new. She entertained the idea for a minute, and then decided that she would do exactly that.

She had been fantasizing about what Jamar Washington possibly had in store underneath all that fine man meat and thuggish but still semi-professional exterior, and she found herself growing aroused at the thought that tonight she would finally see for herself. She exited the restroom now, almost completely forgetting about the tension that was all over her mind just five minutes ago, and headed to the employee locker area, reached into her locker, which had her name written on a sticker outside of it, and grabbed her purse and water thermos. She passed by Jeff, who was speaking with Joose near the deli section. As she headed out, he looked at her expectantly. "Hey, Jeff, I'm not feelin well, I'm gonna go home early today, kay?" Jeff held up a finger to Joose as if excusing himself from the conversation, "Is everything alright? What's wrong?" Jeff asked, clearly wanting more of an explanation as to why she was leaving early. Iesha, who was still walking and did not plan on stopping, halted in her step and turned around to face him. Feeling extremely irritated at his nosey prodding, she almost spat out disrespectfully but caught herself, "I'm just not feeling well, okay…I mean, after everything that happened earlier, surely you understand Jeff….." She softened her tone at the end of her statement as she remembered that she was speaking to her boss. Jeff nodded in understanding, "Yes, Iesha, I do understand. Go on home and get some rest, hon', we'll see ya Monday." He lifted his hand and waived goodbye. Iesha turned and continued walking out with no further response. She was glad to be leaving and looking forward to her exciting plans for the evening.

Chapter 13

Ruthless was in the driver's seat of the Chevy Suburban going 75 miles per hour; he was high on the Cocaine, which was supposed to be given to Shawalli's clique. His head was spinning, and he didn't know what he was doing or where he was going; all he knew was that he and his two underage co-conspirators had crossed a major line, two major cliques, and there was no going back. The three teens had been living on the road for close to one week now, staying in various hotels and eating at different restaurants, constantly on the watch because they figured that they were being hunted. It seemed that the situation was so fragile that they were only living for the day and living in the moment. They had all been splurging, spending up the drug money going shopping for clothes, liquor, additional drugs, and even women; somewhere in the back of each one of their minds, they all knew that it would be coming to an end any day now. Might as well live it up they all agreed.

Ruthless was doing all he could to focus on the road ahead; he was driving on the Business 80 freeway heading toward Reno, still out on the West Coast. He figured that once he reached Reno, they could get a room near one of the casinos in the busy city, and maybe they would be harder to find. With him being the oldest of the three, he had spent more time in the presence of Doctor Willy and Dirty Black, and he knew that more than likely, there was already a crew headed to California in search of them. He reached into the passenger seat, grabbed the bottle of Remy, turned it up, and took a long, drawn-out guzzle of the strong, bittersweet liquor. As he did so, he let his gaze travel to the rearview mirror into the back seat at Lil Rick and Alonzo, who were now both knocked out of sleep from the endless hours of snorting Cocaine, drinking hard liquor, partying, and living on the road. As he looked at them, he noticed how childlike both of them still appeared to be, and a part of him felt guilty that he was the head of this horrible masquerade.

His mind flashed back to the day when he first proposed the idea of robbing Shawalli to Alonzo and Rick. "Man, we can do this. Imagine what we can do with all that money and fly (what they called the snort at times). We can skip to another state and kiss Jersey goodbye, neva look back Yo'…neva look back." He recalled as Alonzo looked at Rick then back at him, "Dude, is you crazy? Doc would have a whole crew lookin fo' us and when he catch us…man, we would be lucky if we was still able to use our legs! You know how he do, I'm not feelin' it man…Count me out!" Then Rick chimed in, "Yeah, Ruth, Lonzo is right, man, but you gotta' point too; if we do get away, we may be able to flip this money, move to a new state and get us some workin' girls and finally be out of havin' to run for Doc and them like we some damn slaves, ya dig?. Man, I'm wit' it, I say let's do it!" Ruthless recalled how he felt his pulse quicken at the thought of them really carrying out the plan; he remembered how a small part of him felt like he was setting them all up for suicide, and the feeling was intensified at the fact that Lonzo was so hesitant. Out of the three of them, Alonzo, though he was the youngest, was also the most level-headed of the crew. He had a way of looking at things from an optimistic point of view and making you open your mind to possibilities that you may not have thought of previously. "Man, I don't know about this one kid. I got a bad feelin' in my gut yo', why don't we just play it cool, keep stackin' our money from puttin' in work, and try to skip out like that?" "Man, you know how long that's gon' take?" Ruthless spat out in a harsh, cold tone that made Alonzo slightly drawback. "While we sittin' up takin' all these penitentiary chances makin' Doc and Black rich we ought to be doin' somethin' to try and free ourself's, you feel me?" As much as Alonzo did not want to admit it, he knew that Ruthless did have a point, but on the other hand, he also knew that if they got caught, they would be tortured and killed. He also knew that they were jeopardizing their families by doing this as well because the first place Black would send people looking would be to their homes.

Ruthless continued to drive down the freeway, passing the city of Auburn; he passed a sign that read Reno 100 miles, so he knew he had a little over an hour to go until they arrived. He was still unsure of what they would do when they got there. He figured they would begin their plans of looking for some working girls and then try to recruit them. They had been trained by Doc and Black on exactly how to do this. Ruthless continued to lightweight map out his plan as he drove; part of him was drowsy and ready to crash due to the days and nights of steadily moving and steadily worrying, while the other part was so wired and amped up due to the drugs he was high on, that he probably would have been unable to sleep if he was afforded the opportunity to do so. He slowly approached a Travelodge motel to the left up ahead; even though he was amped up, being that he had not rested in days, he decided to pull over just to get a quick rest so that he could make it the rest of the way. He had only planned to rest for maybe half an hour or so as he pulled into an empty parking space and cut the car off; he pulled the lever on the side of the seat to recline it back, and after only five minutes, Ruthless was snoring just like his other two accomplices. Even though his body was drop-dead tired, a part of his mind still stirred in restlessness. His thoughts bombarded him and turned into a merging nightmare; he saw himself running down a long, dark street, being chased by someone unseen. In the dream, three shots rang out from an automatic pistol. He ducked and then was stung by searing pain in his side; he fell to the ground as he screamed out, "Aaaahhhhhh! Aaaahhhhhh! Pleeeease, please don't kill me! Aaaahhhhhhh!" The perpetrator was right over him now with the gun aimed at his face. "Git' up! Git' up, I said, right now, boy!" Immediately, Ruthless' eyes popped open as he awoke from his dream, only to see that a bright light was shining into his face. A baton tapped loudly on the window, "Git' up right now! Auburn Police, open the door!" Ruthless sat there still trying to shake off the details of the dream and convince himself that he was still dreaming, but he wasn't; even worse, one of the huge bags of Coke was right next to him in the passenger seat along with the bottle of Remy, which was half gone. The police officer banged on the window with his flashlight as he yelled out one final commandment, "This is yur last time, I said open the door!" At this last commandment, Ruthless shifted his seat back straight up and rolled down the window a tiny crack, "Yeah, officer, what's goin' on? How can I help you?" The officer continued to shine his light on Ruthless's face, blinding him. Then, he proceeded to shine the light inside the truck and on the faces of Alonzo and Lil Rick, who were still sleeping in the back seat. "Can I see your license, registration, and insurance?" The officer asked in a very strict tone of voice. "Officer, may I ask why? What is the reason that you are interrupting me while I'm resting?" Ruthless countered, trying to challenge the officer. "Hey, I'll be the one asking all the questions right now, boy, and I said, where is your license, registration, and insurance?"

Ruthless' mind began to race as he thought quickly about his next move. He did not have a license, and he could not show the registration because the vehicle was stolen from New Jersey. He also knew that when he reached for the glove box, the officer would surely zero in on the drugs which were sitting directly in the passenger seat next to him, halfway covered with his sweater... and if the officer pulled out his pistol, it would all be over; he would have no choice but to get out of the truck and surrender. Ruthless had a small plan that hit his mind in a flash, for him being criminally minded while still so young, he was used to thinking on his toes. He slowly began to reach toward the glove box as if he were going to grab the registration. Then, all of a sudden, he threw his head back against his driver's seat and began shaking and convulsing as if he were having a seizure. The officer stepped back a couple of feet and watched Ruthless for a second, trying to determine what exactly was going on. Ruthless was making choking noises from his mouth and was now deliberately making white foam out of his saliva and causing it to spew from his mouth and onto his chin. The officer immediately ran back towards his patrol car, which was parked about ten feet away to the left of the Chevy to call the ambulance and back up because, at this point, he was convinced that he was watching a genuine epileptic having a seizure which sometimes could happen when intense pressure or stress was being applied to an epileptic individual. As soon as the officer had reached his patrol car, Ruthless quickly turned the key in the ignition, slammed the truck in reverse, and then sped off, peeling out into the opposite direction, causing his tires to squeal and thick grey smoke to cloud behind him.

The officer immediately radioed for backup as he did his best to recite the truck's license plate that he did not take the time to write down and gave a hurried description of the three black male suspects, "10-5! 10-5! I have a black Chevy Suburban with New Jersey license plates, possibly a stolen vehicle with three black male suspects. The suspects fled while I attempted to check regi and insurance; I need all vehicles in pursuit; suspects heading Eastbound on Bus-80 copy..." "Copy 10-5, all vehicles in pursuit." The dispatch operator chirped. The officer was so angry that his entire face was red; he quickly jumped into his car and turned on his lights and sirens, and began speeding off in the direction that the youngsters had just driven off into. "Wake up, ya'll! Wake up!" Ruthless was yelling in the back at Alonzo and Rick; they both began to stir but were still asleep in their drug-induced, almost comatose-like loss of consciousness. Ruthless knew he needed their help to get rid of the dope before any cops were in view of them. He didn't see them in the rearview yet, but he heard the sirens vaguely, and he knew it would be mere seconds before they were in view. He angrily reached back and socked Lil Rick in the leg to wake him, Lil Rick's eyes immediately popped open in fright, "Oww man, wasup' wit you kid, whas' goin on?" Lil Rick asked in an agitated voice. "Man, one time is on us; they pulled over and approached me, so I ran; they gon' be on our trail any second; start dumpin' the fly right now!" Lil Rick began shaking Alonzo, "Wake up, man, wake up!" Alonzo stirred awake to see Ruthless dumping the bag of powder in the front seat out of his driver's side window and Lil Rick dumping two bags at a time out of the back passenger window; he also heard the sirens and began to put two and two together. "Hurry up! Hurry, get rid of it all now!" Ruthless was frantically yelling at the two boys in the back. Alonzo began grabbing bags of dope from the duffel bag on the floor of the back seat; there may have been about eighteen total. Part of his mind couldn't believe that they were doing this, and another part was relieved to think about them in police custody, facing some years locked up rather than having to face the wrath of being tortured by Doctor and Dirty Black. Alonzo and Rick were both ripping the bags open with their teeth, letting the powder blow free out the truck windows and then dropping the empty bags out the window. Rick grabbed two bags, tore holes open in them both, and began turning them upside down outside the window, but suddenly, one of the bags dropped while still almost full of Cocaine. Rick gasped in shock at his clumsiness, knowing that if and when the Police found it, that would be an instant case against them all, and everything they were doing now was almost pointless. He quickly dismissed the thought and continued grabbing bags and pouring out dope. At this point, the first cruiser was in eye view of the rearview mirror and was no doubt able to see the boys pouring the dope out the windows. "How many left?" Ruthless yelled to the back. "Only two more!" Alonzo said as he grabbed them both, ripped the bags open, and held them out the window. The white powder flew out everywhere, and then he dropped the last two bags. Officer Gibson, who was the original officer to approach the boys, was now only thirty feet behind the Chevy; he began to speak into the intercom, "10-30, 10-30 I'm in pursuit New Jersey license plate 5J236FK, the suspects seemed to be emptying bags of white powder out of the truck windows, more than likely narcotics, alert all units over copy...." "Copy that". The dispatch operator chirped back. Ruthless smashed on the gas and took the truck as fast as it would go, tipping over 100 miles per hour on the odometer. He looked back in the rearview mirror, and now he could see at least three police cars behind them, all with their lights on and sirens blaring. He began to really panic as the fear and reality set in on him that they really had nowhere to run to and nowhere to hide. Still, Ruthless pushed his foot down harder on the gas pedal; the big truck was shaking and rattling as it was being pushed to maximum speeds. Alonzo and Rick silently sat in the back and occasionally turned around to glance out the back at the police cars in pursuit.

"Damn! I told you we wasn't gon' get away with this! Why you don't neva' listen to nobody, Ruth!" Alonzo yelled out at Ruthless as he placed both of his fists on each side of his head in frustration. "What's gon' happen to us? What we gon' do now? You know we not gon' get away from these pigs...they all over us!" Alonzo was shaking his head in disgust. "Shut the hell up, man! You aint makin nothin' better. There aint nothin' we can do now but keep runnin', I fo damn sho' aint gon' just give up and lettem' have us...Not without a fight!" Ruthless yelled back at him while watching him from the rearview mirror; he let his gaze travel from Alonzo to Rick and then to the still-pursuing cop cars behind them. He knew that they really had no chance to escape, and even though they had no evidence inside the truck with them, he knew that the cops had seen them dumping it out and would no doubt have crews to collect at least a few of the empty bags that still contained the residue and fingerprints for evidence. His mind desperately raced with crazy ideas about what he should do now; he hated that he was the one who was leading them on this psychopathic masquerade. Just then, Lil Rick spoke up, "Man, Ruth, I say let's pull off the freeway, ditch this truck, and just try our luck footin' it Yo'...... I mean, they just gon' keep on chasin' us, and we aint gon' get away from them in this truck. We gotta' betta' chance just goin' fo' our own on foot." Ruthless just listened without response. He was actually just thinking the same thing to himself, but he really didn't want to split up with his other boys; he couldn't escape the fact that he felt somewhat responsible for their lives. At that moment, a crazy thought hit his mind. It was a dangerous plan, but it may work to get the cops off their trail long enough for them to run and lay low someplace. Without saying a word, Ruthless pulled all the way to the left-hand lane; the cops were still on his trail and were now only five feet behind him; most of the other freeway traffic was a good thirty feet or so behind due to the police pursuit. Still going at a high rate of speed, Ruthless instantly swerved the big truck to the right and began to make a U-turn. Officer Gibson, who was directly behind them, had to slam his brakes to keep from crashing into them, and the cruiser directly behind him slammed into his rear. The rest of the cop cars began to slam on the breaks as well, which caused a chain reaction of burnt rubber, smoke, and cars leering to the left in the middle of the freeway. The wheels of the Chevy lifted up on the right, and all the boys screamed out as it looked for a minute like the truck might tip over somehow amazingly, the truck paused in mid-air and then fell back to its original position; it swerved from the right to the left then completed the u-turn. Ruthless drove through the oncoming traffic doing about ninety miles per hour in search of the nearest exit, which would be on his left.

Cars and trucks were swerving to get out of his way with horns blaring and people cursing with their mouths wide open in surprise and disbelief that the bold criminals would attempt such a desperate move in an effort to outrun the police.

Chapter 14

"Daddy! Look!" 15-year-old Destiny anxiously walked up the steps proudly holding forward a piece of paper, which D'wayne could already tell must have been some type of test. She looked just like a miniature version of her father, slim, slender, and already over 5'8", which was very tall for her age. "Look, I got 100% on my physics exam... Look!" D'wayne held out his arms to embrace his daughter and the good grade that she had received on a difficult test. "Oh, baby... I told you it wouldn't be that hard for you; I knew you could do it!" D'wayne was sitting on the front porch in his rocker, which was his favorite thinking spot. His wife had not gotten home from work yet, and his son was slowly strolling up behind Destiny in his usual quiet manner. D'wayne held one arm around his daughter's shoulder for a few moments and then tenderly kissed her forehead before releasing her as she strode into the house with a merry bounce to her step. D'wayne Jr. slowly lifted his feet to climb the stairs as if he were feeling hesitant about coming home. "How was your day, son? Anything good happen?" D'wayne tried to sound as upbeat as possible. His son had been having trouble adjusting to his Freshman year of high school and had to deal with some of the other kids in the Sophomore and Junior grades teasing him and bullying him. Being that D'wayne and his wife were quiet, church-going people, they did not condone violence, and he had done his best to give his son peaceful solutions on how to deal with the cruelty of the school kids. Jr., who was now

13 years old going on 14, looked up into his father's face and forced a smile, "It was okay, Dad." He also looked so much like his father in his facial features and stature that it was like he spit him out. D'wayne grabbed his son into an embrace and held him for a minute. He admired his son's strength, and he knew that today must have surely gone like most of the other days with the cruel children at school but that his son was not letting it get the best of him.

D'wayne had been planning on doing something spontaneous for his family and taking them on a getaway. It was Thursday, the school was out the next day due to a teachers' in-service day, and he did not have to work weekends, and neither did his wife, which was a luxury that they both fully enjoyed. It would be the perfect opportunity to take off because his family would have three whole days to themselves before they had to be back home for work and school. As he released his embrace on his son, he looked him in the eyes and grabbed both of his shoulders. "How would you like to take a special trip this weekend?" D'wayne expectantly looked into his son's face. Jr. shrugged his shoulders as he looked back into his father's excited eyes. "A trip.....where to, Dad?" He asked as a small amount of wonder began to fill his face. "I'm thinking of taking you to the place where I grew up in New Jersey! Then you can see my old school, my old church, my neighborhood, and the house I grew up in; we can even visit the mall and my favorite old museum! You can learn all about who your Dad was when he was your age... what do you think, son? How bout it?" Instantly Jr.'s face sparked a hint of excitement, which he tried to mask as he calmly asked, "That sounds like a plan, when we leavin?" "Well, I haven't talked to your momma' about it yet, so let's see how she feels about it first, and if all is well, we will head out tonight." "Okay," Jr.

responded as he walked away in the direction of his room. D'wayne sat back down in his rocker on the porch, and as his son trailed off, he imagined what it would be like to be back in Newark again, even for a brief visit.

Years had passed since he had entertained the thought of going back to see his other children, and as time went on, he finally abandoned the idea, but not completely. Somewhere in his mind, he visualized himself driving past his old home just to see if Sheilah still lived there, if nothing else. He thought that she may have moved somewhere else after all these years; he often wondered about his children, who were all grown by now. Damion, the youngest, turned 18 years old a few months back. D'wayne had been gone for 16 whole years, and now his mind and heart were both to the point that they had grown equally numb concerning his past. He had discovered long ago that pushing any thoughts of his other wife and children out of his mind was the only way he could live day-to-day life without hating himself to the point of wanting to die for the huge and scandalous lie that he had created out of his life. To pretend that they didn't exist was really the only way that he was able to deal with it at all. But here, lately, a nagging curiosity had been growing and slowly festering inside of him to go back. He wasn't sure why or what he was even going to be looking for or expecting, but all he wanted to do was go back. He stood up from his porch rocker to check on the dinner he had started nearly an hour ago. On days like today, when he finished his work early and got home before his wife did, he would usually begin the evening meal. It was about 3:30 pm, and he was almost finished with the meatloaf and gravy, seasoned mashed potatoes, green bean casserole, and buttermilk cornbread. He knew that April would be coming through the door at around 4:00 pm; he was excited about the idea for the trip that he would be presenting to her while they ate dinner; he hoped that she would not think it suspicious that he would want to head out to Newark so suddenly this evening.

As he stirred the mashed potatoes, he thought about different ways that he could present his idea to her. He figured that maybe he should just tell her that he missed his old neighborhood and wanted to see how much it had changed. He knew that she was not the argumentative type, and she had never had a reason to suspect anything about him, so there really would be nothing else for her to do but agree to the plans. He looked in on the meatloaf, casserole, and cornbread in the oven and saw that it was done, so he turned the oven on warm and took another glance at the kitchen clock. It was now 3:55, he felt his pulse quicken at the excitement and adrenaline he felt surging within his body, and he wondered why he was feeling this way. Deep inside his heart and mind, he knew that even visiting Newark was wrong based on the secret that was buried there. Part of him thought about canceling his decision, but the other part, the curious part, was in high gear of his consciousness, and besides, he felt that he had put this trip off for long enough as it was. Just then, the living room door slammed, and April was home. "Ooohhhhweee som'n smells delicious! What you cookin', Mr. Turner?" April jokingly called out in her usual light manner of humor as she entered the kitchen. D'wayne looked up from the potatoes on the stove and went over to his wife. He wrapped his arms around her, and the two shared a passionate kiss. D'wayne smiled as he ran down the menu to his wife, "Baby..... we got some of my gourmet meatloaf, with signature gravy, herbed mashed potatoes, my famous green bean casserole, and, you guessed it! My one-of-a-kind buttermilk cornbread, uhhm uhhm uhhm!" She continued to hold him in her arms as she smiled and rocked back and forth in anticipation of the evening meal. "Uhhm it sounds yummy, and I'm starvin' too, so when we gon' eat?" April pulled away and picked up her purse from the floor. She began to head toward the back of the house, where D'wayne told her he would be serving their plates momentarily. When she came back out from the bedroom, all four of their plates were sitting on the table piping hot, her two darling children were seated next to each other, and D'wayne was standing as usual behind her chair, which he had pulled out for her to take a seat. As April sat down to the wonderful meal, she was again reminded of just how lucky she was to have a real gentleman in her life. He had not changed one bit from how he was 16 years ago when they started their relationship. To this day, he even pulled her chair out for her before they sat down to eat and always opened doors for her no matter where they were going or what they were doing. As she sat down to her plate, D'wayne took his seat right next to her, and everyone bowed their heads to pray before eating. "Father God, bless this meal, may it nourish our bodies and strengthen our spirits in Jesus' holy name, Amen!" "Amen!" Repeated April and the children. They all began to eat in silence as D'wayne gathered his words regarding the trip. Just then, Jr. looked toward his father and asked, "Daddy.... did you tell her yet?" April and Destiny both looked up at Jr. and then toward D'wayne. April took her napkin and wiped her mouth, "Tell me what, Suga?" D'wayne was caught off guard as he shot an irritating look over at his son, whose response was simply to look down at his food and continue eating in silence. "Uh honey, I was gonna see how you felt about hopping on the highway, being adventurous, and taking a little trip tonight and heading toward my hometown, Newark; I've been wanting to go back and visit just to see how things have changed since I left." April just looked back at D'wayne in silence for a moment without speaking. She wasn't the type to question her husband's decisions, but she did wonder where this must have come from; it did not seem like something a person would want to do out of the blue. "Well, sweetie, it doesn't sound like a bad idea, but you want to travel over 900 miles just to see how things have changed over the years?"

D'wayne had momentarily forgotten that he had lied about being in Newark all the way up until right before he moved back to Georgia. He realized at this moment how difficult it was to maintain this lie, as he quickly pondered on the stories he'd told his wife when they'd first met, of being overseas in the military and how it had temporarily escaped his mind, and he had forgotten that according to him and his parents, he had not been to New Jersey since he graduated from high school. He didn't realize how crazy this all sounded from his wife's point of view. Why was he interested in revisiting his childhood stomping grounds of all places?

April neglected to respond right away as she silently looked back at her husband in an almost concerned type of way. D'wayne looked down at his food as he struggled to find an alternate explanation. This was one of the many times that he wished he could just come clean and clear his conscience of the filthy secret that had held him captive all these years, but he knew it was something he could never bring himself to do. He looked back up at April, who was still watching him with eyes that were searching for an explanation, "April honey, to tell the truth, I've been feelin' a lil' homesick here lately for some reason, and I sort'a wanted to just go back and maybe check up on a few friends and maybe see if they're still around, you know?" D'wayne had not completely thought out his response, and now that the words were out, he couldn't believe that he was allowing the situation to head in this direction. Now if they did go, April would be looking to see who he wanted to go back to Jersey to see. Reluctantly, she nodded her head, "Alright baby, if it will make you feel better, I say let's do it! We can start packin' up after dinner; it's fine with me." April smiled and looked at her husband, still wondering about the worried look on his face. As much as she loved him, she knew that there was more to the story than what he was telling her. Still, she had never been the suspicious type, and she was not going to start being that way now; she knew her husband enough to know that he always had his own reasoning for doing whatever he did when he did it, and besides, she thought, a getaway would be good for all of them.

After dinner that night, the family began to pack their bags for about three days worth of traveling; the children laughed and squealed with delight in their rooms as they put their outfits and bed clothing inside of their duffel bags. They packed their shoes, socks, and underwear in accordance with their mother's constant prompting every few minutes, "Kid's, don't forget your toothbrushes" and "Don't forget your bath towels and washcloths." April stood inside her bedroom with her bag completely packed. She absently gazed out of the window as she thought to herself about the fact that D'wayne had never really spoken very much about his hometown to her or the children, and anytime she asked about his childhood, he would answer her with a vague and general answer which provided no real specific information at all. Maybe this trip would be a good way to get her honey to open up about his childhood.

April found herself recalling a time when D'wayne had said something she felt was off-key, and it stuck inside of her mind even though she dismissed it at the time. When Destiny was only five years old, she played in the front yard on a hot summer's day. She had been trying to teach herself how to use summersault when she finally got it. She had her very first perfect summersault, and she was overjoyed and excited, jumping up and down and screaming, "Mommy!...Daddy!...I did it! I did it!" She recalled how D'wayne had jumped up and ran out into the yard and picked Destiny up; holding her tight, he swung her around and around as they both laughed. When he finally let her go, they both stumbled for a moment due to being a little dizzy, and as soon as Destiny's dizziness wore off, she was right back at it, doing her now-perfected summersault. D'wayne came and took his place next to April, absentmindedly saying, "Ohhhh...she's just like Iesha." April recalled how she immediately became alarmed, but she held her cool as she calmly asked, "Honey, who is Iesha?" D'wayne snapped his head around and looked at April in such a way that she had never seen before and had never seen him do since that day. His expression was that of surprise and what also looked like fear as he began to stammer, "I...I...Iesha was one of my younger cousins; she...she passed away some time ago." D'wayne quickly spat the words out as if they tasted bitter in his mouth. April looked at him with regret on her face as she apologized. She remembered how the expression on his face slowly turned into that of hurt and pain, and after a few moments, he got up and walked into the house without excusing himself like usual. That awkward moment had stayed on April's mind for years, but somehow, she allowed herself to tuck it all the way to the back of her mind, and she stopped thinking about it, that is, until now; here she was, reliving that day as if it were yesterday and for the first time in years, wondering about who Iesha possibly really was, and what had she meant to her husband. Could she have been an ex-girlfriend? Then again, she could actually be his long-lost dead cousin... after all, she had never known her husband to lie to her about anything- she had no reason at all to doubt him.

"Suga' are you all ready?" D'wayne came up beside April and laid a soft hand on her left shoulder. April allowed her thoughts to subside as her gaze fell down upon D'wayne's hand and his wedding band, which was surrounded by his hairy fingers; she kissed his hand and then replied, "Yeah baby, I'm all packed and ready to go...I'm excited, too! Are you ready to hit the road?" She smiled at her husband and turned to hug him, "Yes honey, I'm all packed and ready; I think this trip will do me good; there's a part of me that wants to see my old home for one last time....." The couple headed out of their bedroom holding their bags and called the kids, who came running out of their rooms with their bags packed, as they eagerly ran outside to the car. D'wayne glanced at the clock on the living room wall, which read 5:50 pm, as he closed the door behind him and locked it. If all went well and the traffic was good, he reasoned they should arrive in Newark at around 2:30 am; from there, they would book a room at the Rob Treat Hotel for their three-day stay. It was a perfect location near the mall, the Newark History Museum, and downtown. His family would have a good time being shown around the city, and he would also drive them past the church that he used to attend and show them the neighborhood he used to live in. He figured he would maybe knock on a couple of random doors and pretend that someone he knew used to live there so that it would appear to April that he had a valid reason for wanting to make this long drive to Newark and that he could at least make it like he wanted to see a couple of people in particular.

As the family hit the road and drove off, D'wayne turned on the radio, and recognizing one of his favorite songs, he began to sing along with it. Destiny surprised him by joining in. The whole family had an upbeat vibe, and the excitement of reaching Newark began to set in on them as they entered the freeway on-ramp, reading the sign that read New Jersey 945 miles. April's gaze traveled out the window and at the beautiful country scenery of the city passing behind them as they headed out; she wasn't sure what this trip held in store, but she felt a nervous anticipation inside for a reason that she wasn't sure of. She laid her head back on the headrest and did her best to get comfortable and put her uneasiness aside as she reminded herself that her husband loved her with all of his heart and would never hide anything from her or try to do anything underhanded to her in any way. As the highway unfolded before them, she found herself dozing off.

Chapter 15

C-Low felt as though his head were going to burst open. He didn't know what he could do in this situation, but he knew he had to do something; he couldn't go out like this, just buckle down and let this pig take him to jail without a fight, he wasn't having it. As the officer finished reading him the last of his rights C-Low quickly squatted down on the floor and swung out one of his bony legs that flew from beneath him with lightening fast speed and he swept his leg beneath Officer Tyson and caused him to trip flat on his back, and hit his head on one of the steel poles that stood right behind him causing him to lose consciousness momentarily. The whole thing happened so suddenly that Officer Tyson had no time to react the way he had been trained in the academy to handle such a situation. As he fell on the floor, his gun flew from its holster and slid onto the ground right next to C-Low. C-Low hurriedly twisted his scrawny legs inside of his arms, bringing his cuffed hands to the front of his body, and grabbed the pistol off of the floor. He then pointed it at Jackie, "See, bitch, I tole you that I was gon' git chu...didn't I?" C-Low growled as he held a wide grin displaying his crooked and rotten teeth. "Whatchu gon' do now, biiiitch... You ratted on me? Huh? You ratted, and thawt you was gon' git away wit it too didn't ya?" C-Low was now wagging the gun back and forth as he inched toward Jackie; she was so frightened and horrified by the sudden turn of events that she was unable to do anything except sit in one place, frozen and staring at C-Low in unbelief. Part of her wanted to get up and run as fast as she could, and yet the other part of her was paralyzed with fear. "I...I didn't tell on ya...I promise I didn't 'C', I would neva..." Jackie's small and puny voice trailed off as C-Low quickly lunged toward her and busted her in the face with the butt of the gun. "Shut up slut! Don't try to essplain yo' self to me...I already know what time it is, go ova' there and git them dam keys of that pig so you can unloose these cuffs offa me!" As she felt the blast of pain in her nose, she immediately grabbed her face in both hands and let out a loud, painful moan. While holding her face, she felt the first few familiar trickles of blood begin to seep out, and then it began to gush forth like a hot volcano erupting. For the first time in a long time, it occurred to Jackie that she really was better than this and that she truly deserved a better life for herself. She began to experience an emotion rising up within her that she had never felt before, it was a combination of frustration, repulsion, hate, and revenge, all balled up in one, and the most notable of all was fury; it started in her chest and began to consume her in way she had never thought possible. Jackie hurriedly scampered over to the still unconscious Officer Tyson, who lay on the floor just beginning to stir; she knew that the only chance of her escaping alive was to outsmart C-Low. She tried to give the appearance that she was desperately looking for the set of keys by searching the officer's pockets, but in reality, from her view, she could plainly see that the keys were still attached to the officer's service belt. Just then, as she began to feel helpless and that her only chance of escape may have been to take off running on her already bloody feet, she noticed on the small table just to the right of her the gun that Officer Tyson had taken from his jacket. The gun was only two feet away from Jackie; she knew that she had to make a split-second move. In an instant, Jackie hurled over Officer Tyson and grabbed the 45 off of the dresser, and pointed it steady at C-Low's face. To her surprise, she wasn't shaking or afraid; she looked him square in the eye with an expression of pure hatred that was so intense it could have burned a hole right through him. Jackie slid the barrel back in preparation to fire as she had seen C-Low do so many times before. C-Low's eyes were wide with fear and shock; he couldn't believe the expression that was now playing on Jackie's face. He honestly did not believe that she had any kind of a backbone in her body, and he never thought the day would come when she would stand up to him. The blood continued to run down Jackie's face and onto her shirt, coloring her lips and the rest of her face in a way that made her resemble some sort of Aztec warrior; combined with the look in her eyes, C-Low felt himself growing afraid of her for the first time since he had known her. "Drop the damn gun....." Jackie growled in a barely audible voice. C-Low only stood there looking at her, as a part of his mind was busy trying to assess if she could possibly be bluffing or if there was actually a true threat of her firing the pistol and shooting him. Jackie immediately aimed at his hands and fired the gun. A bullet skimmed C-Low's wrist, and he dropped the gun as he loudly screamed out in pain, "Aaaahhhhhhh! You dirty bitch! How could youuuuu, afta all I done did for you? Ahhhhhh Aaahhhhhh!" C-Low Screamed out in pain.

   Officer Tyson's eyes immediately snapped open at the loud sound of the gunshot being fired so near him, "Okay, Miss...... give me the gun. Don't make a mistake that you'll regret for the rest of your life; he's not worth it. Give it to me." The officer held his hand out to Jackie as he literally begged her to hand over the gun, C-Low was now crumbled down on the ground holding his still handcuffed right wrist with the other hand as blood spilled out in a thin stream onto the floor. "No!" Jackie screamed out in pain and fury. C-Low's wide eyes darted up at her as she spoke. "I been takin' his shit fo years and I aint gon' take it no mo! I should kill you dead, you sorry nigga! All the hell you done put me through! Damn you!" Jackie fired another shot at C-Low as he screamed and rolled to the left. Just then, the tent curtains were snatched open, and two additional officers ran in with their weapons drawn, "Drop the gun now, or I'll be forced to shoot!" a female officer ordered Jackie. The other officer rushed over to Officer Tyson, who was still sitting on the ground and holding the back of his head, which was bleeding, in a semi-disoriented state. Jackie, who seemed to be glued to one spot, did not even look in the officer's direction; she couldn't seem to remove her eyes from C-Low as the hatred and anger burned through her soul. "Ma'am, this is your last chance; I said drop the gun!" The officer ordered one last time; she cocked her service weapon in preparation to shoot. "No, don't shoot...Let me talk to her; she'll listen to me." Officer Tyson yelled out while holding his hand in the air in the direction of the officer holding the gun. "Please, please put down the gun..... I promise you, he's going somewhere that he will be for a long, long time, and you don't want to be in the same predicament, think about your future.... you said you wanted better, right?" Jackie finally took her angry gaze away from C-Low, and looked around at Officer Tyson, "Yeah...I do want betta' fo myself...I really do." She turned and handed the gun to Officer Tyson, who was now standing right behind her. The first female officer came and lifted C-Low onto his feet as she began to escort him outside to the patrol vehicle. The other officer began taking statements from both Jackie and Officer Tyson, who decided to press charges against C-Low. The charges ranged from assault with a deadly weapon, assault, and battery on a police officer, as well as possession of an illegal firearm and being in possession of stolen goods. Officer Tyson looked Jackie in the face, and for some reason, his heart went out to her in a special way. She reminded him of his Aunt, who had fallen victim to the vicious streets of New Jersey when he was only a child; she died so young due to chasing drugs and the fast life. Now that he was a police officer, he did his best to help people who found themselves in situations like these if he could. He cleared his throat and began to speak, "Now, why don't you begin by telling me your name." Officer Tyson grabbed a notepad and ink pen from his front pocket. Jackie allowed herself to drop her guard a bit, taking a few deep breaths as she looked around the tent, realizing that she may be looking at it for the last time. She looked back into Officer Tyson's eyes... and responded in a small voice, "Jackie... Offissa... my name is... Jac... Jackie Whitman..."

Chapter 16

"Listen up, Garden Projects Mafia! We are facing a serious hood situation." Doctor Willy was now addressing the gangsters of Garden Projects. He had hoped it wouldn't go this far and that the stupid youngsters would come back home with at least some of the drugs and money, if not all of it. It had been eight days now, with no word at all from the threesome that he had dispatched out to California to handle the hoods business. He and Dirty Black had already sent thugs to search the boy's friends and relatives homes,' and the word back was that they were nowhere to be found, so from there, a crew of five thugs was sent to California to find the boy and then kill them. He had been trying to keep this silent from the rest of the clique until absolutely necessary, and now, apparently, the time had come. They had woken up this morning to the sounds of explosions going off in the rear of the apartments. Shawalli had sent some ugly messages by having five cars blown up and a few black stuffed dolls hung by nooses in the trees that lined the parking lot. As soon as the Doctor and Black heard the explosions and ran outside, they knew that this was Shawalli's way of announcing that his clique was bringing a war against the mafia. It had been years since another clique had dared to try and test the mafia. Every hood knew how deep they were and that they had gangsters that spread out all across the state, but in this situation, Doctor and Black were almost equally fearful of the notorious Afghani street lord Shawalli and his bloodthirsty clique who seemingly killed for fun. Doctor was now angrily holding his pistol in the air, "I want every one of ya'll to get yo' gat's and all yo' weapons cause it's goin' down tonight! We gon' ride or die on these fool's, ya'll understand?" "Yaaaaahhhhhh!" The mafia yelled out and screamed as they cheered in favor and rowdy anticipation of the war going down. Doctor Willy turned to walk back inside his apartment while still clenching his fist. His gun was now in his waist, and he was holding his shoulders in a tense, squared position as he walked, which he only did when he was ready to kill someone. It was rare to see Doctor in this type of a state because he had long abandoned his killing days and left that up to the Baby G's and other gangsters of the mafia. When Doctor was this upset it was best not to say anything to him or get into his way. Dirty Black turned to follow him without saying anything; he knew with the war going down tonight that the clique was going to need all the ammunition they could find. Pistols, rifles, grenades, shanks, and G's that had pledged allegiance to the mafia for life even though they didn't come to hang out anymore; he thought about one in particular, one who had made himself into a legend from being so hardcore......Bloody Boy Joose.

◆◆◆

Joose stood with his hands in his pockets, listening attentively as Jeff finished thoroughly explaining his job responsibilities, "You will also be responsible for making sure all of the doors are locked before closing, keeping the isles clean of trash, and cleaning up any spills or messes that may occur." Jeff's voice faded out as Joose started getting lost in his thoughts. He couldn't believe all of the events that had happened today and that he was finally in one of those spots that he believed was the right place at the right time.

He was still a little shaken up by the gun being pulled on him and the encounter with the bum, but now, look, he had finally landed a job. Jeff told him that he would begin by making $9.50 per hour, full-time, and he could begin on Monday. He was going to have a uniform made up with his name on the front pocket, and he would officially be the store's security guard as a primary position, but he would also have to help with stocking and general store cleanup. Joose knew that he could handle it, and as hard as he had tried to find work since he had been out, he definitely was not about to blow it for himself; he already had it made up in his mind that he was going to work hard and truly impress Jeff, in an effort to make him glad that he had hired him. He also felt he had a point to prove to Iesha, who did not want to help her own cousin; he was still a bit bothered by the expression she had worn on her face when Jeff announced that he was considering him for employment. He knew hateraide when he saw it, and it was definitely hateraide in the third degree, but why? He just couldn't put his finger on it; he had never done anything personally to Iesha, and he had never given her a reason to dislike him, period. It was bothering him, and he felt he would have to address it with her before he started working on Monday; maybe after church on Sunday, he thought to himself; just then, Jeff's voice interrupted his thoughts, "So what do ya think?" Joose's gaze re-focused on Jeff's face as he answered in a low tone, "That sounds real good, sir; thank you so much for giving me a chance like this; I can assure you, you won't be sorry."

Jeff smiled in response, "I'm sure I won't be, and please call me Jeff; everyone at the Food Mart is like family, so all I can say is: Welcome to the family!" Jeff advanced near Joose with his arms extended as if to hug him, but Joose was immediately alarmed at his gesture and suddenly stepped back. Jeff stopped in place as if feeling embarrassed and let his arms drop to his sides, "Sorry, I get a little too excited sometimes when we hire new people on board...well, anyway, unless you have any questions for me, I guess we'll be seeing you Monday morning at 10:00?" Jeff nodded his head and held his hand out for a handshake; Joose reached out and grabbed Jeff's hand, shaking it in an extra firm grip as he returned the handshake and confirmed, "I'll see you Monday at 10:00." Joose turned to walk out of the Food Mart and fought with all of his might the urge to turn around and look at Jeff to see if he was watching him walk out, he knew he probably was. Joose felt so excited; he was smiling and did not even realize it until someone passed him walking and looked at him in a strange way; he couldn't wait to go home and tell G.G. and Pop the good news. He even figured his baby brother would be happy for him as well. He began to pick up his pace as he walked and imagined the look displayed on his grandparents' faces when he told them that he had just been hired to work at the Food Mart as the new security guard. He decided that he wouldn't even tell them about the drama that happened and how his job was won as a result of it. As he turned the corner, he could now see his grandparent's home coming into view, but as he took a few more steps, he saw a familiar Lime green old-school Cadillac pulling away from the curb of his grandparent's house and skidding away, making a loud noise as it sped around the corner. Joose quickened his pace and began a light jog. He knew that the Cadillac appeared to be owned by Dirty Black, but he knew that they never came to this end of Newark. Still, he could not deny what he had seen as his heartbeat began to pound harder; he felt a knot growing in his gut at the knowledge that more drama was beginning to brew.

As he reached the house and turned his key inside the lock to go in, he felt someone on the other side forcefully push the door back shut and put the chain lock in place. "What's goin on? It's me G.G, Pop, open up!" Joose pounded on the door a few times with his fist. "We told you, Joo, you besta' not bring none of dat' gang stuff to our house or else you had to go, but you just couldn't listen, could ya'?" Pop yelled out from behind the door, "You gon' have to get outta' here, we aint gon' have none of dat' nonsense at our house, no sireeeee!" "Pop, I aint had nobody come to the house! I got more respect for ya'll then to bring them thugs to the house, Pop I told you I'm threw with all that, please believe me? I didn't have nobody come, please Pop, open the door....." Joose pleaded as he lightly still pounded his fist on the door and looked down in frustration. This was all he needed, it seemed as soon as one good door opened for him, another tried to shut in his face. This time literally, and after a few moments, he heard the chain sliding back across the lock, and the door opened back up with Pop standing in the doorway holding a small piece of folded paper, and G.G. standing off to the side with a worried look on her face. "If you aint involved with that gang no mo' Joo then explain to us what this is posed to be about then!" Pop thrust the note to Joose, and he caught it as the small paper bounced off of his chest and began falling toward the ground; he looked up at Pop then slowly began to unfold the small piece of paper; it read: Watup Joo! We all been waitin for you to make yo grand appearance to the projects, you know how we do! Theres a urgent situation goin on in the hood, and we need you to come and assist us with some fonk we got, so don't u dare leave yo peeps hangin! Come thru soon as you get this-

Black. Joose read the note with a bitter scowl on his face, and as he finished reading it, he balled it up in disgust and threw it into the street with all his might. He couldn't believe this was happening, what was he going to do now? The fact that Dirty Black had come in person to his grandparents' house sent a threatening message in itself on what the possible repercussions could be if he did not comply. He couldn't see himself going back to the mafia and putting in any more work; he was completely done with that, and at the same time, he knew that once you joined a gang like the Garden Projects Mafia, the only real way out was death.

Chapter 17

Ruthless swung a quick and reckless left turn as the trucks large tires rolled and bounced over the curb as a result of him entering the off ramp going the wrong way. His adrenaline was pumping and his heart was beating so fast that he thought he may have a heart attack even at the young age of 17. He found himself thinking that the initiation that Doc gave him had come in handy, and he felt his mannish pride swelling from within him at the realization that he had successfully and momentarily shook the cops. He knew that he had to think quickly because with the way that the five police cars were pursuing them it would be only a matter of precious minutes before they would be on their trail again. He drove speeding down a main street that was off of the freeway, and felt a small wave of relief as he saw a shopping mall coming into view, and what looked to be a residential neighborhood directly behind it. This would be perfect for them he reasoned, now they could ditch the truck, run through the shopping plaza and jump the fence; and they were more than sure to find either a vacant house or even an apartment complex that they would be able to hide out for a while. Ruthless continued to press the gas pedal, pushing the truck to 80 miles per hour. Alonzo and Rick sat quietly in the rear, both obviously worried about the situation that they had gotten themselves into. None of them had outwardly spoken of the fact that they were already as good as dead anyway, because they knew without a shadow of a doubt that Doctor and

Black already had hit men looking for them out here on the West Coast. Only now did they each realize that they must have been absolutely insane to believe that they would get away with a major cross like this. To make matters worse now all of the Fly was gone, and the money was dwindling day by day, on general living expenses. Rick was the first to break the silence, "Ruth, were you goin man?" Ruthless continued to smash on the gas pedal as he now approached the shopping complex, he swung into the parking lot with a loud screeching noise as the truck swerved and the tires burned rubber on the asphalt. Ruthless began to feel excited as he spotted a parking garage to the left of the shopping center, he quickly navigated the parking lot until he made his way to the entrance, and as he pressed the button to get his admittance ticket he heard the first loud sirens and in his rearview mirror saw three police vehicles speeding down the street going past the shopping center.

He drove around the twists and turns of the parking garage, feeling comforted that it was so packed he couldn't find anywhere to park on the upper floors, so he had no choice but to head to the basement. He found a spot in the back as he hurriedly pulled into it, shut off the truck, and laid his head back on the head rest in relief. After breathing deeply for a moment, he decided to answer Rick's question. "Son...I figure like dis'... let's go through this mall and act like we shoppin' around, so we can buy ourselves some time, and then let's make our way through that neighborhood that's right behind us and we can lay low maybe till we can get another car or somethin." Both Alonzo and Rick began nodding in agreement. "You thank its still cool for us to head toward Reno, Ruth?" Alonzo asked him as he scratched his head. "Yeah, man...that was the plan, wasn't it?" Ruth spat out sarcastically while still doing his best to sound confident. On the inside, however, he was probably more afraid than both of the younger ones put together and for the first time in a long time, he seriously regretted that he was supposed to be the leader of the bunch. Furthermore he found himself truly realizing that he had made a grave mistake by choosing to have them cross Doctor and the Mafia. He constantly thought about what they would do next, and each felt the steady realization that nowhere they could run to was safe. Ruthless opened the driver's side door and got out. Alonzo and Rick did the same, but not before Alonzo grabbed the backpack full of money from behind the rear seat; then, they headed toward the basement floor elevators, which would lead them into the mall. Each of them was feeling uneasy in the present circumstances. Alonzo's heart was beating rapidly; he hated feeling like this because he knew the feeling was pure, raw, and identifiable fear. It was a well-known topic among gangsta's that you were never supposed to be afraid; no situation, person, place, or thing was ever supposed to pump fear into your heart, period.

    They entered the elevator and pressed one for the first floor; as the elevator accelerated upwards, it added to the already queasy feeling in Alonzo's stomach. He felt like something horribly wrong was getting ready to occur. He knew that they were in a terrible no-win situation, but there was something else; he just could not put his finger on it. Finally, he spoke out, "Hey Ruth, man....somethin' ain't right. I got this feelin' that we should a stayed in the truck. I...I don't know bout this kid..." Both Lil Rick and Ruthless turned to Alonzo and noticed the look on his face. They both knew that Alonzo was a little more cautious than the two of them, but he still had never been the scary type. They both noticed the look of fear in his eyes. Lil Rick tried to comfort him, "Lonzo, its gon' be aight man...just try to chill, we gon' make it..." He then slapped him on the back in a light manner. Ruthless looked at the two younger boys with a sour expression on his face, he then sneered his mouth to the side and tried to come back in his usual tough boy manner, "Man... quit actin' like a beeeyach! You know the situation, we gotta do what we gotta do, and that's all! Man up, Son!" He said this as he pounded one fist on the front of his chest in an exaggerated manner to show off his own apparent manhood. A bell made a chiming noise to alert them that they had reached the first floor. The elevator doors opened up, and they all exited. The mall was so busy with people that it looked to be the perfect place to hide out for a little while, and they would have had no trouble blending in, except that the majority of the people there just so happened to be of the opposite race. There were white families, couples, and teens hanging out, seemingly happy and laughing with what looked to be no cares in the world whatsoever. As the three boys looked in either direction they were apparently thinking the same thing as they noticed maybe two or three other persons of color in the entire mall that they could see within eyeshot. The three boys stuck out like sore thumbs as they began their awkward walk through the mall. They began receiving weird looks and stares from everyone that they passed; they figured that it was just from the color of their skin, but in reality, it was that fact coupled with the obvious that they were not locals, and they looked really rough in appearance from their days and nights on the road with hardly any rest. Ruthless displayed a head full of wild and unruly dreadlocks; he was tall and meaty and appeared to be much older than his seventeen years of age. Lil Rick was short, brown-skinned, rather handsome, and looked his age, but he was covered in tattoos and even had some small ones on his face: a tear dropped underneath his right eye and a small heart with a crack going down the center of it near his left eye. There was a look of roughness displayed in his eyes that told a story of tragedy and loss. Alonzo was possibly the most innocent looking out of them all; he was obviously young and looked as if he could be 10 or 11 years old and not 13. He was skinny and short and wore his hair in a short afro, which was lined up pretty neatly; he did not have any tattoos yet, and looking at him, a seasoned gangster would have known that he was just really getting his feet wet with learning how to live a criminal lifestyle. He was only one of hundreds of the young runaway boys that Doc had makeshift adopted and had begun the transformation of turning him into one of many money-makers for the hood. They continued to stroll through the mall as they did their best to ignore the uncomfortable stares that they were receiving. Ruthless, who was very outspoken and arrogant, simply stared right back with an unspoken expression of 'What the hell you lookin' at?' displayed on his face. They were almost to the exit when, all of a sudden, they heard gunshot blasts and one of the huge windows they were walking past shattered. Bang! Bang! Bang! The three quickly looked around and spotted five young black men about three stores down, with guns drawn and aiming at them; instantly, they knew that they had been found by Doc's henchmen, and the hunt that they had so desperately been praying was not going to happen was finally upon them. "Run! It's Doc and them boys! Run!" Ruthless yelled out in a loud voice. The three boys broke into a mad run, with Doc's boys chasing them at a fast pace. As screams rang out people everywhere started madly running in all directions, they made their way out of the doors to the mall and toward the residential area that lay just past the parking lot. As they ran, they heard gunshots ringing out at a rapid pace and felt the bullets that were whizzing past their ears and apparently barely missing them. All of a sudden, Lil Rick fell to the ground as he screamed out in horror and pain, "Ahhhhhh, I'm shot! I'm shot!" Alonzo shot a quick look back at him and saw him lying on the ground and screaming, holding the back of his thigh in pain; he continued to run all the faster, knowing that this was life or death that each of them was facing. He hated to leave him but he knew that Lil Rick was good as dead now. Ruthless did not even waste the time to look back; he already knew what Lil Rick's fate would be. After Lil Rick fell, the gunshots halted, but after a few moments had passed, a single gunshot sounded, and the screaming came to an end; both of the other boys knew that their friend had been killed.

Both Ruthless and Alonzo continued to run wildly toward the fence that was at the back of the parking lot. More gunshots were being fired, and now they hit the fence and sent wood splintering and shattering into the air all around them. Alonzo reached the fence first and began to climb over it; he was just getting over the top when he heard Ruthless scream, "Ahhhhh... Ahhhhhh...." Alonzo looked down to see Ruthless crumpled on the ground with his kneecap bleeding; he was still reaching toward the fence. The mobsters from Doc's click were less than 20 feet away; Alonzo continued to run as he heard Ruthless begging for his life. "No... Please don't kill me, No!" Then, two gunshots rang out, and he heard the screams and pleas of his friend Ruth go silent. Alonzo knew he was now completely alone and running for his life. The thugs were not going to stop until he was dead. Alonzo was now on a residential street, and he jumped the next fence, which led into the backyard of the first house he came to; he ran around the side of the house and slowly twisted the doorknob, and to his surprise, it came right open into what looked to be the garage. There was an older Cadillac parked with lots of dust over it. Alonzo quickly slid underneath the car, and he did his best to breathe quietly while struggling to catch his breath. He had not prayed in so long, but he found himself silently praying now, "Please God, help me... I don't wanna die; I'll do anything... please..." He felt close to tears at the reality setting in on him that he was being hunted ferociously and that his two fellow partners in crime were now dead. What would he do? Where would he go now? He held his breath as he heard footsteps right outside the garage, "Where the hell he at, man? He couldn't have gone too far, we was right on his trail!" Then he heard another voice, "Man, he could be in any of these houses, he aint stupid enough to hide in the first one, let's go across the street; he may be still running." He heard the footsteps and voices begin to fade as he let go of his breath and began thanking God for what seemed to be his prayer being immediately answered. He was so tired and exhausted that he laid his head on the ground and began to cry. His tears were a mixture of relief, sorrow, pain, and frustration at his situation. For the first time in months, he thought about his family, which he had left behind when he ran away. He had felt his mother was too strict on him, and his father was way too religious. He wanted a change of pace, so he ran away, and one lonely night, while wandering the streets, he ran into Doc, who offered to buy him something to eat. He was so hungry that he accepted the offer; he thought back to how Doc had seemed so nice and acted as if he only wanted to help him. He never knew that accepting the meal would turn into him owing Doc and him owing Doc would turn into him working for the clique known as Garden Projects Mafia and being jumped into the gang. He had been through so much in the last nine months since he had been gone; he had murdered people, robbed people, and done many other despicable acts that he needed forgiveness for. He now let the tears freely fall from his eyes; they dripped down onto the ground and formed a cold puddle that surrounded the side of his face. He lay there with the tears oozing out of his face, as he felt like his eyes weighed a million pounds. His troubles were far more than he could bear right now, he felt himself slipping into unconsciousness due to overwhelmingly sheer exhaustion. Soon, he had fallen asleep, and when he awoke, it was the pitch black darkness of sometime during the midnight hours outside; he had no idea of how much time had elapsed. He lifted his face up off of the ground as he noticed the numbness he felt from the coldness of the cement he now lay on and the dried tears that he had cried earlier. He began to slide out from underneath the car when it occurred to him almost instantaneously that he still had the backpack full of money strapped onto his shoulders. He felt a small twinge of joy begin to play from deep down inside of him as he felt hope about where he could go from here. While he was asleep, it was as if he were dreaming about being back at home; he remembered his mother's hot-cooked home meals and comforting words that would lull him to sleep at night. He missed being home so badly that he decided at once that he would find the nearest Greyhound bus station and head back home. He climbed to his feet and straightened himself up. He had no idea of what time it may have been, but he hoped that he could at least find an open fast food restaurant so he could buy himself something to eat because he was starving. He knew there was no doubt that Doc's boys were still looking for him and more than likely highly upset that he had gotten away, so he had to be careful. He went to the same door that he had come in through, but not before noticing a small stream of light coming from underneath the door that led to the house; he heard voices coming from inside, which told him that the family was now home if they had not been earlier. He slowly eased out of the side door and hopped the fence, which led him back onto the street in which he had been chased down earlier when he was running for his very life. As he was slowly walking toward the fence that led to the rear of the shopping plaza, he stopped dead in his tracks. He saw flashing red and blue lights as well as a lot of activity bustling from between the slits on the other side of the fence. He realized that the police had been notified about the shooting and were more than likely gathering up the bodies of his former accomplices and no doubt had the entire area covered in yellow tape by now. He turned back the other way and decided to take a detour as he shot up another silent prayer to God that he would not be found by the dangerous thugs that he was sure were still hunting for him. Or maybe not, he thought to himself; it was a strong possibility that they had grown tired of looking for him hours ago and just simply given up. Alonzo walked to the end of the street in a hurried pace, and when he reached the end of the block, he decided to turn a right in hopes that it would lead him back out to the main street. He could see about a mile down that there were cars racing back and forth, which told him that his assumptions were right. He began to feel excited as he thought about how good it would be to be back home with all this madness behind him; he thought to himself that he would more than likely just tell his parents the truth about where he had been all these months and what he was doing.

He would have to explain how he had gotten all of this money, but just then, a fearful thought came to him, which he voiced out loud. "Man, if I tell Pops where I got this dough from, he gon make me turn it into to Police, or get rid of it...You already know he aint gon' allow it in his house." He finished speaking to himself as in third person. Alonzo continued to walk on as he lightweight wrestled with a new possible obstacle, he could lie and say he found it; his parents may not believe him but they wouldn't be able to say for a fact he was lying he thought. He continued to walk, quickening his pace as he decided to deal with that when the time came, but for right now, all he wanted to do was find something to eat and get directions to the nearest bus or train station.

As he finally neared the main street, he stood on the corner, trying to decide if he should head left or right. He saw plenty of shops and stores down either way, but he judged by the lack of activity that it may have been about 2 or 3 AM, which meant that he had better find himself something to eat at a 24-hour spot. He noticed about a quarter mile to the left a big red and white KFC sign, with a big blazing red 'Open 24 hrs' sign right underneath it, so he immediately began to head in that direction. He started walking at a hurried pace, as he became aware of the fact that, on some level, God must have been watching out for him. He quickly thought about how he had never heard of a 24-hour KFC, or maybe it was a Cali thang... he didn't know, nor did he care- he was just so hungry that he began lightly jogging in that direction. When he reached the restaurant, he went inside and was glad that there were only a couple of people sitting quietly and eating. He headed toward the restroom first, and once inside, he used the bathroom, then sat on the stall and opened the backpack to pull out some small bills that he could keep in his pocket for easy access. He took out five twenty-dollar bills and rolled them together, stuffing them in his front pocket. For once, he was thankful that he looked like a younger boy than he really was because this way, no one would question why he was wearing a backpack or what it may have contained. He just looked like a schoolboy who could have had a sack full of books on his back. Not counting that it was late at night. He came out of the restroom and headed toward the counter; as he began to look at the illuminated menu, he felt his mouth-watering, and everything looked delicious to him. His stomach let out a long growl; he hoped the cashier had not heard it. In a high, cheery voice, the young white girl whose name tag introduced her as Chelsea smiled, revealing a mouthful of braces, and told him very politely, "Welcome to KFC. Would you like to try one of our chicken pot pies this evening?" Alonzo quickly turned the suggestion over in his mind and then answered, "No thanks, ma'am, I think I'll get a three-piece with all white meat, mashed potatoes, and a large strawberry soda for the drank." The cashier looked at him from behind her thick glasses and smiled even wider as she commented on his accent. "Boy, your sure not from around here are you?" Alonzo looked back at her and, without smiling, only nodded. He couldn't help but feel irritated at the cashier noticing him because it was the wrong time; he was so hungry he felt like he could eat a dead horse, not to mention he was still paranoid from all the stuff he had been through; he simply wanted to eat in peace and be on his way. "Man...it's not every day that we get out-of-towners in these parts, that's for sure!" Chelsea said as she giggled and put her hand up to her mouth, seemingly forgetting that she was supposed to be taking his order. Alonzo tried to remain calm as he felt his blood beginning to boil; in as nice a voice as he was able to maintain, he said, "Chelsea..... I'm hongry, and I'm tired, could you pleese just rang me up, pleeese?" Chelsea's face slowly began to turn red, and her smile faded; she began to hurriedly punch in numbers into the cash register, and then, in a bitter-sounding tone, she spat out, "That'll be 5.25..." Alonzo took out a twenty from his front pocket, and as he handed it over, he felt a little bad about how he must have come across. "Hey, ma'am, I didn't mean to snap at you. It's just been a long, long day, okay?" Chelsea just looked back at him as she gave his change, still obviously offended, "You just try to have good customer service skills and people feel like your pestering em'." She handed him his receipt and told him his order number was fourteen. He slowly walked away from the counter and sat near a window, waiting for his number to be called. It seemed like forever to him as his stomach continued to rumble; finally, after a few minutes, his number was called. He quickly went to the counter and grabbed his food, sat in the same seat, and removed the plastic lid; he grabbed one of his pieces of chicken and tore into it, allowing the hot and greasy juices to squirt into his mouth as he bit into it. He was chewing so fast that he almost choked, and that was when it occurred to him that he had not eaten in two days. It took him no time to finish the meal and drink his soda, and he finished in less than ten minutes. He got up and dumped his tray, and as he headed out of the restaurant, he passed an older man sitting near the entrance; he asked him, "Sir, would you by any chance know where the nearest Greyhound station or train station may be?" The gentleman gave him directions to continue down the street, the direction he was already taking, and to take a left at the next main street, and he would run right into it. He thanked the old man and headed out.

Milton Keynes UK
Ingram Content Group UK Ltd.
UKHW031324271124
451618UK00015B/381/J